TEMPTING HUNTER

ONCE UPON A FUNERAL

SHERYL LISTER

ABOUT TEMPTING HUNTER

When the powerful patriarch of the Prescott family dies, four brothers are challenged to return to Rosewood Heights and fulfill their grandfather's last wishes. With each of these compelling and complex men facing their inner demons, they must ask themselves if light can shine in the midst of tragedy and if home is truly where the heart is...

Hunter Prescott... A lone wolf thrives off independence and privacy. Yet, even a wolf excluded from his pack can long for something more. Can Hunter shed his protective shield and open his heart to new possibilities?

Tempting Hunter Copyright © 2021
by Sheryl Lister
ISBN: 978-1-7338670-9-2
All rights reserved.

Editor: BR Sutton
Cover Design: Sherelle Green

To all those who believe in second chances.

GAME CHANGER

Hunter Prescott lowered his head and kissed the woman who would become his wife tomorrow.

"Yo, man, this is just the rehearsal. Save all that hot stuff for later."

He glared at his best friend, Mark Russell, then smiled down at his fiancée. "He's lucky we're in the church, otherwise—"

Michaela Saunders placed a hand over Hunter's mouth. "As you pointed out, we *are* in the church." She shook her head, hooked her arm in his and together, they strolled back up the aisle.

Several minutes later, the wedding coordinator gave final instructions and dismissed the large group that had gathered. Hunter's three brothers had all teased him mercilessly about being the first one to fall in love and marry, and now stood off to the side giving him the I'm-glad-it's-not-me look, but he didn't mind. Michaela was worth it. His mother was beyond ecstatic about the possibility of having more grand-children. His sister, Ava—the baby of the family—had married a few years ago and had two children, but his mother been after the rest of them to settle down.

As they filed out into the parking lot, Hunter tripped and nearly lost his balance, something that had occurred more than once over the past few weeks. As the Vice President of Marketing for Prescott Holdings, he'd been working non-stop to get things in place for the new resort opening in Southern California in a year, and had been dividing his time between there and his home in Rosewood Heights, South Carolina.

"Maybe you should stick to having only non-alcoholic beverages tonight, baby. You're already a little unsteady on your feet," Michaela teased. "Mark, make sure he's sober enough to make it down the aisle tomorrow. I've been planning this Christmas wedding for almost a year and I want it go off without a hitch."

Hunter slung his arm around her shoulders and dropped a kiss on her temple. "Everything will go as planned. I'm just a little tired." They'd be spending three weeks in the Bahamas, which would give him plenty of time to relax and catch up on his rest. He glanced down at the sexy woman cuddled into his side. Then again, maybe not.

Mark chuckled. "Don't worry. I'm driving, so he'll be there if I have to throw him over my shoulder and carry him."

He snorted. "Let's get this bachelor party thing over with." He wasn't particularly fond of being the center of attention, but had given in after being badgered by Mark for the past two months. Hunter had been adamant about not having strippers. The only half-naked woman he wanted draped over him was Michaela. "See you tomorrow afternoon at the altar, sweetheart."

Michaela came up on tiptoe and gave him a quick kiss. "Can't wait. Love you."

"Love you, too." He watched her strut across the lot to meet up with her bridesmaids, who had planned a party for her, as well.

Mark let out a low whistle. "You do have it bad."

Hunter shot him a dark glare and strode off toward Mark's car. On the drive to Charleston, he leaned his head back, closed his eyes and mentally went through the marketing plan he'd developed for the new resort, checking off each item, in hopes that he hadn't missed anything. Mark would be handling things in the interim, so he felt confident any issues would be dealt with effectively. He sat up just as his friend parked in the lot of a jazz club. Inside, there were about fifteen men gathered in a private room and they let out a loud cheer when Hunter entered. He just shook his head. His twin brother, Cooper, handed Hunter a glass filled with who knew what, then held up his own.

"Dearly Beloved, we are gathered here tonight to give our final respects to Hunter, who will be departing the land of the freedom in hopes of a better place in matrimony. Let us seize the moment and cram a lifetime of living into the next few hours."

"Hear, hear!"

Hunter touched his brother's glass and took a sip of what turned out to be Jack and Coke. Over the next two hours, laughter and ribald jokes filled the room while the men consumed all manner of food. At the end, only Mark and his brothers remained. Dominic, the oldest, slid into a chair next to Hunter.

"You ready to do this, bro?"

"Absolutely."

Maverick, his youngest brother, clapped Hunter on the shoulder. "Glad it's your ass, and not mine. I'm out. See you tomorrow."

He nodded. "Later." Minutes later, he and Mark headed

out and he waved at his brothers as they drove off. As Hunter reached the car, he fell.

"*Oh, shit!*" Mark was there in a flash. "You good, man?" he asked as he helped Hunter up.

He wanted to say yes, but at that moment, he couldn't move. "I don't think so. I think I need to go get checked out." It took a few minutes, but he finally dropped into the car seat. His arms and legs felt like lead. Mark drove as fast and as safely as he could to the nearest hospital. Not much scared Hunter, but this had his heart beating nearly out of his chest with fear.

After a two-hour wait and a million tests, the doctor came in and his grim expression made the hairs on the back of Hunter's neck stand up. The man started off with some hard to pronounce diagnosis, but the only thing Hunter could process was that his life might never be the same. A wave of anguish washed over him because he knew what he had to do. He could barely lift his arms, but by sheer will got his phone up to his ear. He made the first call to his twin, who would pass along his message to the family. The second call proved to be much more difficult, his only saving grace being that he knew she'd still be at her party.

"Hey, Michaela. Something…" He drew in a deep breath to steady his emotions. "Something came up and I'm…I'm not going to be able to make it tomorrow. Whatever you think, know that I will love you always.

～

One year later…

Hunter struggled through the last set of squats and felt his frustration rising. Fitness had always been one of his top priorities—it not only kept his body in top form, but it also helped keep his stress levels down—and becoming fatigued from doing ten simple body weight squats had him about to lose his mind.

"Great job, Hunter." The physical therapist assisted Hunter onto the chair. "That's it for today. You're doing great and I can tell you've been keeping up with your exercise regimen. I have you scheduled for two evenings next week at six o'clock." She handed him a card with the days and times. The therapist had been very accommodating with scheduling Hunter at the end of her day, so as not to interfere with his work day.

"Thanks." He took a few deep breaths and let them out slowly.

"See you next week." She patted him on the shoulder, gathered her equipment and left him sitting alone in the room he'd set up as a gym. On the heels of her departure, Mark strolled in.

"Just finished meeting with the marketing team and the second ad campaign is all set."

"Glad to hear it." Since that fateful night a year ago, Hunter had been running the business remotely from his home in Southern California, with Mark primarily taking the lead. His friend shared the details of the ad campaign and they went back and forth about the next steps. He opened his mouth to ask a question and his phone rang. He frowned when he saw his sister, Ava's name on the display. His close-knit family had respected his wishes not to call, although he knew it was difficult for them to do.

"Hey, Ava."

"Oh, Hunter, I'm so glad you answered. I miss you so much. Are you okay?"

He could hear her crying and it tore at his insides. He hadn't seen her or his family since leaving. The only person who even knew Hunter's location was Cooper, and he'd only told his brother two months ago. "I'm okay, baby girl. What's going on?"

"Granddad is gone," she whispered. "I wanted to know if you're coming home for the service. Please say you're going to come."

"Damn," he muttered. Hunter had flown into Rosewood Heights a month ago to see the old man after finding out he'd been hospitalized and despite his grandfather's pleading, had left without visiting his family. He hadn't been ready. He still wasn't.

"Hunter?"

"I'll be there." Ready or not, he *had* to go.

THE FUNERAL

Michaela and her two best friends filed into Rosewood Heights Baptist Church with the mass of people who had come to pay their final respects to Abraham Theodore Prescott. The Prescotts were one of Rosewood Heights most prominent families and as evidenced by the near capacity sanctuary, the loss of their patriarch would leave a huge void in the town. She had already been in a funk since Christmas because it marked one year since her non-wedding, and for Mr. Prescott to pass away a few weeks later, let her know this year probably wouldn't be any better than the last one. He'd always asked about her art and told her he couldn't wait for her to become his granddaughter. A lump formed in her throat. *Too bad it didn't work out...for either of us.*

"Do you think Hunter will be here?" her friend, Melanie Johnson asked as the three women squeezed into a row near the back.

A few people nodded her way and she responded in kind. "Don't know, don't care. I have nothing to say to him." She glanced down at her left hand. She had finally stopped wearing her engagement ring, but her finger still bore the tan line of where it used to be. The old emotions tried to surface, but she pushed them back down. Even after a year, the hurt had not faded, but she refused to waste any more of her precious thoughts on Hunter Prescott. She just wished she could erase him from her heart as easily.

She leaned over and whispered to Michaela, "There's the family."

As hard as she tried to keep her eyes focused forward, Michaela couldn't help taking one little peek. No Hunter.

Her other friend, Lana Ward, frowned. "I can't believe Hunter didn't show up for his own grandfather's funeral."

"It's not the first time he's ghosted someone," she muttered.

"Don't you want to know the reason why he left, though?"

"The only acceptable reason he could have would be if he was dead or close to it," she whispered harshly. Michaela let out an exasperated sigh. She did not come here to spend her time talking about the man who left her a voicemail the night before their wedding telling her he wouldn't be there.

Lana nudged her. "Guess he didn't ghost his grandfather, after all. Wait, is it my imagination, or is that a cane?"

"Shh, the pastor is talking." *Do. Not. Turn. Around.* She repeated it to herself over and over, but her traitorous gaze went there anyway. Michaela felt her eyes widen and a soft gasp escaped her lips. Hunter had lost weight and did, indeed, have a cane aiding him as he made his way toward where his family sat. *What happened to him?* She refocused on the pastor, but the questions continued to bombard her for the remainder of the service.

After the service ended, Lana drove them over to Rosewood Estates for the repast. Michaela wished she had driven her own car, so she could've skipped the whole thing, but she was at Lana's mercy and had to endure seeing the man who'd shattered her heart once more. She made sure to keep him in her line of sight so she could stay as far away from him as possible. And she'd done a good job of it until now. He stood only a few feet from her talking with his brothers. As if sensing her scrutiny, he turned her way. Their gazes locked and in his eyes she thought she saw regret and something else she couldn't name. Yet after all the pain he'd caused her and the anger she still felt, he still had the power to make her heart skip a beat. And that pissed her off even more. Giving him her best go-to-hell glare, she pivoted and strode from the room. As far as she was concerned he could go back to whatever hole he'd been in...*forever*.

❧

Hunter did his best to ignore all the stares and questioning looks from people who had come to his grandfather's repast. He'd thought about ditching the cane, but with the estate filled beyond capacity, falling on his ass would guarantee more than just *looks* and he didn't want anybody in his business. He tuned out Dominic grilling him about not letting the family know where he'd gone.

"And what's up with the cane? What happened to you? We could've been there to help."

He met Dominic's scowling face. "Dom, you of all people know I don't like to be smothered, and I'll tell you all about it later at the house." It had been hard enough going through the hell that had been his year, but no way would he have been able to deal with the pitying looks from his family or his mother and sister's tears. *That* he could not handle. So he'd done what he felt was best and what he'd always done—deal with it alone.

"We're all meeting at the house after this for the will reading," Maverick said.

"I'll be there." Fatigue had become his constant

companion and right now, he needed to find some place to rest, preferably in a bed. He hadn't been inside his condo in over a year and, although he still paid someone to come in and clean once a month, Hunter didn't have so much as a stick of chewing gum in the place. And at this moment, grocery shopping was out of the question.

He turned to leave and there stood Michaela a few feet away. His heart rate kicked up just like it had the first time he'd seen her at an art festival three years ago. His gaze roamed over her cocoa face. In the time he'd been away, she had become even more beautiful. When their eyes met, she gave him a glare so cold, he actually shivered. Not that he'd expected anything different. Hunter released a deep sigh and headed toward the exit.

By the time he got to his car, he'd decided to book a room at the town's inn. It was a short five-minute drive away and solitude it offered would fit the bill perfectly. The young man at the front desk recognized Hunter and booked him into one of the suites on the first floor situated in a more private area. As soon as he entered the room, he undressed and fell across the bed. He was asleep before his head hit the pillow.

Two hours later, Hunter awakened feeling somewhat rested. He made it to his parents' home a few minutes before the lawyer began the will reading. His mother rushed over and grabbed him up in a crushing hug.

"Oh, baby, I'm so glad to see you." She palmed his face and eyed him critically through her tears to be sure he was okay, just as she'd done when he was a little boy. "I can't believe you've been gone all this time and you've lost so much weight…the cane. Honey, are you okay? I think you need to come back home so I can take care of you."

Back home to live with his parents? Oh. Hell. No. Brenda Prescott loved her children to distraction and would give her life for any one of them. But he hadn't lived at home since leaving for college at age eighteen, and now at thirty-seven, it was definitely not an option. "Whoa, Mom. I am not moving back home. I can manage on my own." He heard the snicker from his smart-ass brother, Maverick and shot him a look.

"I don't even know what happened to—"

Hunter grasped his mother's hands. "Mom, I promise I'll explain before I leave for LA." He and Cooper shared a look. Cooper had kept Hunter's secret and respected his decision not to accept any help, even though Hunter knew how hard it had been for him to do it.

His father entered with the attorney and detailed the procedure for the will reading. Apparently, Granddad had videotaped his personal messages for his family. Going in birth order, Hunter was third in line, being four minutes younger than his twin. The knowledge that he'd never see the old man again, sent myriad of emotions swirling through his gut. When Hunter had visited the hospital, Granddad took one look at Hunter and the first words out of his mouth had been, "Your ass looks like you need to by lying next to me." Hunter heard his name and tuned back in to his grandfather's voice.

"Hunter, I want you to oversee the commission of a mural to be painted in the new cancer treatment wing at the hospital." His grandfather's generous donation had been responsible for the new building. "That place is so drab, it's a wonder anybody can survive," Granddad continued in his matter-of-fact speech.

A smile touched Hunter's lips.

Granddad's face turned serious. "And, son, it's time to come home. I understand how much you crave your privacy, and doing things on your own, but the good Lord didn't make us to go it alone. That's why he gave us family. Your family loves you, Hunter, and it's time to come home." He waved a weathered hand. "And before you get your drawers in a bunch, I'm not telling you to relocate back to Rosewood Heights. I'm talking about your heart. Don't forget what I told you when you came to see me."

Every head whipped in Hunter's direction and he met the accusatory stares from his family. *Thanks, Granddad. That visit was supposed to be between you and me.*

"Bring your heart home, Hunter."

Once they'd all been addressed, the attorney went through the rest of the will related to properties, monies and his grandfather's personal possessions. Granddad had left Hunter the painting of a sunrise Michaela had done to hang in his hospital room with a note that read: *Let this be a reminder that every sunrise is an opportunity for a new start. Make each one count.* Once the attorney finished and had gone, their father stood with several white envelopes in his hand.

"I also have something for you all. Your grandfather wrote you each a personal letter with strict instructions that you read them and do as he requested. Your inheritance is not contingent on this, but these are his final wishes."

Hunter was still stuck on his grandfather's final words. *Bring your heart home.* He had no idea what that meant. He absently took the envelope that had his name written across the middle in his grandfather's familiar handwriting. His siblings all slowly tore into their envelopes and he followed suit.

Hunter,

You have an amazing eye when it comes to art, which is why you are the perfect one to handle this project. I've already cleared the way with the hospital board for the artist I've selected—Michaela. Of course, Tom wanted his daughter to be the one to create the mural and is going to do everything in his power to create problems. But I have no doubts you can handle him, if necessary. Make sure she has whatever supplies she needs. I know

Michaela will do me proud, as will you. I'm including two numbered envelopes for you to give to her.

Son, I know life threw you a curveball and you've endured a hell of a year, but I also knew that if anybody could overcome the odds, it would be you. You've always been one who went after whatever you wanted, particularly with business. It's time to do the same in your personal life. Get yourself together and do what's best for your heart.

Granddad

P.S. She's the one for you. Fix it.

He glanced at the other two envelopes that had a note stuck on the front with the specifics of when to give them to her. Hunter recalled the earlier frost from Michaela. *How in the hell am I going to get her to even talk to me, let alone work together?* As far as her being the one for him, yeah, he agreed. However, some things couldn't be fixed. But Hunter loved his grandfather and knew he wouldn't deny him his last wish to have the mural done. He'd make it happen, no matter what.

CHAPTER 1

*M*ichaela underestimated how much seeing Hunter would affect her. Twenty-four hours later, she still couldn't get him out of her mind and as a result, had been awake since five on a Sunday morning, instead of sleeping in. Restless, she'd spent the past four hours trying to do everything she knew to relax. Nothing worked. Not the stress-relieving candles she'd lit throughout her home, nor her playlist of string compositions by Black Violin. So many emotions swirled in her belly—anger, confusion, curiosity, and somewhere buried in a deep, dark corner...love. It was the last emotion that infuriated her. How could she still feel anything near *love* for a man who claimed to love her, but walked away without a backward glance? She'd tried not to imagine him in the arms of another woman, but she couldn't shake the notion. The embarrassment of that day rose up all over again, but she shoved it aside. As she'd told herself yesterday, Hunter Prescott wasn't worth one more second of her time or her heart.

She rolled her head toward the clock sitting on her nightstand. *I've been lying here for almost five hours.* Flipping the covers back, Michaela got up, dressed and headed to the area of her condo she'd set up as an art studio. Painting had always been her escape, the calming place where nothing existed outside of her and the canvas. She desperately needed that space today. She'd begun work on a sunset view of the lake on Rosewood Estates after visiting a week ago. Michaela closed her eyes and visualized the colors, the sounds, the feelings. *He stood behind her, his arms wrapped around her waist and his lips trailing the fleetest of kisses along her neck and bare shoulder. She shivered.*

Michaela's eyes snapped open. *Ugh! Why am I thinking about this man again?* Somehow, her mind dredged up a memory of one of the many times she and Hunter had spent there. Obviously, seeing him had triggered something within her subconscious and she wanted, no needed, it to stop. Trying again, she inhaled deeply, let the scent of chamomile and lavender fill her nostrils and put her brush to the canvas.

She startled when her doorbell rang. *Probably Lana or Melanie, or both.* Michaela had purposely not answered their calls last night, knowing her friends wanted the answers to questions to which she had none. Sighing, she wiped her hands on a towel and went to answer the door.

"You know if you two—" She pulled it open and the words died on her lips. *Hunter.*

"Hey."

"What do you want?" Michaela couldn't believe he had the audacity to show up as if nothing had happened.

"May I come in? I need to talk to you."

She opened her mouth to tell him where he and his *talk* could go and he held up a white bag. She didn't even have to guess what it held. She smelled the fragrant blueberry muffin from Roseberry Bakery. Her favorite. And he knew it. *Damn him.* "Fine." She stepped back to let him enter. Hunter handed her the bag and she tried not to snatch it out of his hands. *Mmm, it's still warm.* Her stomach growled.

Hunter walked over to her half-done painting. "It's good to know you're still painting." He angled his head one way, then another. "The lake on the Estate. I like this. Even though it isn't finished, it looks so real, as if the water is going to spill out over the canvas."

"Thanks," she mumbled. He'd always been supportive of her art and often encouraged her to pursue her dream full-time. Not wanting to take another trip down memory lane, she asked, "What do you want to talk about?" Michaela tried not to be moved by his deliberate steps aided by the cane. Instead, she opened the bag, broke off a piece of the muffin and popped it into her mouth. She stifled a moan and glanced up to find him watching with a quiet smile.

"I know you like them hot out of the oven, so I waited for a fresh batch."

An awkward silence crept between them. "Um...you can have a seat." Michaela waited until he sat on the sofa, then took the furthest chair away from him.

"Did you come here to try and entice me with the muffin for whatever you came to say or is this an attempt to try to make up for the mess you caused?" Hunter's dark, penetrating gaze bore into hers and she almost squirmed in her seat.

"No, Michaela. I came to talk about Granddad. We can talk about us another time."

"There is no *us*," she snapped. Regret filled his face, but she ignored it. Or at least tried to do it. She shoved another piece of muffin in her mouth and waited for him to speak.

"Granddad made a request in his will to have murals painted in the new oncology wing the hospital just completed. He'd like for you to do it."

Michaela almost choked. She coughed to clear her throat. "What? Why me?"

"Why not you? You're a brilliant artist."

Being commissioned for such a large project would be just the opening into the art world Michaela had been looking for and would, no doubt, provide other opportunities. She might even be able to finally quit her job at the bank to pursue art full-time. Inside, she turned cartwheels and did a little drop-it-like-it's-hot move. Suddenly, warning bells went off in her head and she paused her party. She gave Hunter a wary look. "Hold up. What's the catch?"

Hunter frowned. "I don't know what you mean."

"There are five of you and you're the one delivering this message. Why not Ava, or one of your other brothers, or your father? Or even the attorney. Why. You?"

He paused briefly. "Because I'm the one you'll be working with on the project."

"What?" She jumped up and started pacing. *Ohh, nooo, I cannot work with him. But then I'd have to pass on the biggest opportunity I've ever had.* Needing to find her happy place again, she grabbed up the bag from the table and stuffed more of the muffin in her mouth, grateful it was large enough to hopefully help her regain her equilibrium. She could *not* deal with Hunter on any level, especially after what he'd done to her.

"Those were his orders. Believe me, I was just as shocked as you are when I found out. I know this is hard for both of us," he said softly. He paused as if trying to steady his emotions. "But I intend to honor his last wish, and because you cared about him, I'm hoping you'll do the same."

"I need to think about this. Hey, it's the best I can do under the circumstances," Michaela added when she heard him sigh.

"That's fine." Hunter stood and handed her an envelope. "He asked me to give you this."

She accepted it and saw her name scrawled on the front. "What is it?" Curiosity made her want to rip into it right then and there, but she kept herself in check, afraid that the contents would impact her in a major way. And she didn't want to read it in front of him.

He shrugged. "I have no idea. Give me a call and let me know what you decide." He started for the door.

"I don't have your number."

He paused with the door half open but didn't turn around. "My number hasn't changed."

"Then I guess that means you were ignoring my calls or too busy to answer all those times I tried to reach you after you dropped off the face of the earth," she said sarcastically.

Hunter slowly rotated to face her. "Believe me, it's not because I wanted to," he said, pain lacing his words. "I'll see you later." He walked out and closed the door softly behind him.

Michaela dropped back down in the chair. Angry tears burned her eyes. She tapped the envelope lightly against her forehead, then slid her finger beneath the flap to open it. Changing her mind, she tossed it on the coffee table and rubbed her hands up and down her thighs. "Don't be a wimp. Just open it," she muttered. But she couldn't. Hopping up, she went back to her painting. *Believe me, it's not because I wanted to.* His words played over in her mind. What did that even mean? *Why did you have to come back?*

∿

Hunter parked in his parents' driveway and sat there for a few minutes to get his bearings. The impact of being in close confines with Michaela and feeling her anguish had broken his heart all over again. He'd asked himself over the past two days whether he would have done something differently if given the chance again, but knew he'd make the same choice because he loved her. He hoped one day she could understand and forgive him. Scanning the large structure in front of him, he tried to prepare himself for another emotional confrontation. If he'd had any sense, Hunter would've postpone the visit for another time, but in twenty-four hours, he'd be on a plane back to California.

He drew in a fortifying breath, got out and went inside, where he found all his siblings sitting around in the living room talking. "Hey." His brothers nodded. As he knew she would, Ava rushed over to him.

"Where've you been? I was worried." Ava hugged him around his waist and laid her head on his chest.

"It's before noon, sis." He kissed the top of her hair.

Her husband, Owen, clapped Hunter on the back and gave him a one-arm hug. "What's up, man? It's good to see you."

"Same here."

"Now that we've gotten all the greetings out of the way, what the hell happened to you?" Dominic asked. "And Cooper, why didn't you tell us?"

Cooper shot Dominic a glare. "He asked me not to and I don't tell people's shit."

"I'd rather just say it once," Hunter said.

Maverick, lounging on the end of the sofa, waved a hand. "Then bring Mom and Dad in here, so we can hear it."

Ava rolled her eyes and ran a comforting hand up and down Hunter's back.

Hunter knew this would be difficult. Dominic's scowl hadn't changed since Hunter walked in the door. Wanting to delay the conversation as long as possible, he asked, "Where are my niece and nephew?" As soon as the words left his mouth, they came barreling around the corner. Hunter hadn't seen them in over a year and his heart nearly beat out of his chest with love, excitement and fear that they wouldn't remember him. Little Sully—what the family called Owen, Jr. because he was a replica of his father—had grown from a chubby baby to a little boy, and looked undecided about Hunter.

"Uncle Hunter!" Madison rushed over and wrapped her little arms around his legs.

"Be careful, Maddie," Ava said.

"It's okay," Hunter said. He'd braced himself for the contact. He bent and kissed her cheek. "How's my favorite girl?" Not trusting himself to pick her up, he sat on a chair and pulled his niece onto his lap. She'd gotten taller and he knew she'd started school.

"I'm good. I missed you. How come you were gone so long?"

"Maybe she'll be the one to get the information, since we can't," Dominic drawled.

Hunter bit back the sharp two-word retort poised on the tip of his tongue. "Maddie, I was sick for a little while, so I couldn't get on an airplane to visit. But I'm better now, so I'll be back to visit soon."

She launched herself against him. "Oh, goodie. You can come to my house tomorrow."

With her smiling at him so expectantly, he couldn't say no. "Just for a short time, okay. I have to catch a plane tomorrow." Apparently pleased, the little girl kicked her legs happily. Little Sully, finally deciding that Hunter was safe to approach, came over and extended his arms. Hunter picked the toddler up and placed him on his other leg.

"Oh, my goodness. You look like such a natural holding them, Hunter."

He glimpsed over his shoulder to find his mother

standing across the room with misty eyes and a trembling hand over her heart. "Hi, Mom." He usually stood to greet her, but with both children taking over his lap, he thought it safer to stay seated.

"Don't get up," she said perceptively. She crossed the room with the elegance and grace of a queen and kissed his cheek. "How are you feeling today?"

"I'm fine. Just getting reacquainted with these two."

"Uncle Hunter's coming to my house tomorrow, Grandma," Madison announced.

"That's just wonderful, sweetheart. Your father will be here in a moment."

Hunter saw his twin get ready to open his mouth and gave him a look. Cooper and their father had been at odds since forever and Hunter didn't have the strength to play referee today.

Ava came over and gathered the children. "I'm going to get them settled in the family room with a movie. I'll be right back."

"Hunter, how are you, son?" Edward Prescott, entered the room, his commanding presence filling the space.

He stood and embraced his father. "I'm good, Dad."

"Okay, I'm back. What did I miss?" Ava asked as she rushed back into the room and claimed a seat on the sofa next to her husband.

"Nothing," his mother said. "Hunter?"

Every eye turned his way. Knowing he couldn't hold off any longer, he leaned forward, clasped his hands together and bowed his head. Granddad's words filtered in his mind. *Let the family in, Hunter.* "When we were leaving the bachelor party, I fell and couldn't move. Mark took me to the hospital and after lots of testing, the doctor said I had something called polymyositis. It's an inflammatory muscle disease and started causing weakness in my legs and arms, then progressed to the point that I couldn't move at all." Hunter closed his eyes, recalling the stark fear that had gripped him, the depression and the constant "why me" questions that had dominated his mind.

"Dammit, Hunter! We should've been there," his father said, running an agitated hand over his head.

"Apparently, Cooper was there."

Cooper threw up his hands and scowled at Dominic. "Look, I've only known for a couple of months, so no, I wasn't there. Can we move on?"

His mother came and sat next to Hunter and slid an arm around his shoulder. Hunter didn't have to look at her—or Ava—to know they were crying, and Prescotts never cried. But he drew strength from the arm that had always provided comfort while growing up. "I couldn't handle the pity and I didn't want any of you to see me that way." It had been hard enough for him. The first time he'd seen himself in the mirror had shocked him and sent him spiraling so deep into depression he didn't ever think he would be able to climb out. "I was in the hospital for several months and when I came home, had twenty-four hour care. I had to learn how to do everything again—walk, dress, *everything*."

"I can't even imagine," Maverick said. "So, this...*happened* just like that." He snapped his fingers.

"No, you can't imagine, and I wouldn't wish this on my worst enemy. It wasn't something that happened spontaneously. My best guess was that it had been going on for about a year. The fatigue I thought had to do with my long work hours was actually the part of disease."

Dominic raised an eyebrow. "But you're up and around now, so you're cured, right?"

"There's no cure, but thank God, with the medication and therapy, my recovery has been..." He trailed off as his emotions engulfed him, once more.

"It's been a miracle in my eyes," his mother said, hugging him close. "Is there anything you need us to do to help you, Hunter?"

"You're all here. That's all I need right now." He met his family's gazes and knew that no matter what, he'd have their support. The room fell silent for what felt like forever.

"Grandma, when are we going to eat? I'm hungry."

Everyone spun around at the sound of Madison's voice and his mother said, "As soon as we finish talking to your uncle, okay, honey?"

"Uncle Hunter can you be finished, so we can eat?"

Hunter laughed for the first time since that horrible night and it felt good. "Yeah, baby girl, I can be *finished*." Besides, the conversation had emotionally drained him and he needed five minutes to himself. A grim feeling settled in the pit of his stomach when he remembered that, at some point, he would have to have the same conversation again. With Michaela. Somehow, he knew it wouldn't go as smoothly.

CHAPTER 2

*H*unter sat on the sofa in his sister's home Monday morning reading with Madison. She'd been glued to his side from the moment he got there. Any fears he'd had about her forgetting him had disappeared. Even Little Sully had warmed up to him enough so that the two had spent a little while playing with Sully's toy cars.

"Are you going to be gone a long time again, Uncle Hunter?" Madison asked, her little face filled with concern.

"I might have to be gone for a while, but I'm coming back. Remember, we talked about it yesterday at Grandma and Grandpa's house yesterday. And I'll call you sometimes and we can talk on a video."

"On Mommy's iPad?"

He lifted a brow.

Ava, who had come into the room, chuckled. "These are twenty-first century technology babies. They're born knowing how to work electronics. Even Sully knows how to find his kiddie games on a tablet."

"I've really been out of the loop. Maddie, I guess we'll be talking on Mommy's iPad."

"Yay!" She jumped off the sofa and took off.

"Madison Sullivan, *walk*," Ava called after her.

Hunter smiled.

She came and took the spot Madison had vacated. "You're a natural with them. I was hoping I'd have my own little niece or nephew to spoil by now."

He didn't know how to respond, so he didn't. He and Michaela had talked about having children—at least two, and she often teased him saying they were going to have to start right away so he wouldn't be too old to play with them. Now, more than likely, it would never happen.

"Have you had a chance to get into the details of what Granddad wants for the mural? I know some local artists if you need a name."

He shook his head. "He wants Michaela to do it."

Her eyes widened. "*Your* Michaela? Are you serious? I mean…*wow*."

Hunter's thoughts exactly. "I wish I wasn't, but those were his instructions, and apparently he's already gotten the board's approval. So…" He shrugged.

Ava fell back against the sofa. "I don't even know what to say. I'm really surprised because everybody in town knew what happened and I'd think Granddad wouldn't want to put either of you in that kind of situation. Have you talked to her since…since…you know? I saw her at the repast and noticed that she couldn't keep her eyes off you."

Most likely because she was trying to make sure their paths never crossed. "I saw her, too."

"Did you try to talk to her? I thought it was nice of her to come. I know Granddad had already begun to think of her as his granddaughter."

So he'd said. "I went by to talk to her yesterday. Let's just say I made it out alive and leave it at that." Michaela still hadn't called him to say whether she'd do the mural and in all honesty, he couldn't blame her, especially with him appearing out of the blue after dropping off the face of the earth, as she'd put it, and without even offering an explanation. But being near her, had tempted him to touch her and see if her skin was still as soft as he remembered.

She shifted to face him. "Hunter, you're my brother and I love you, but I can't believe the way you just left her like that. I was pissed at you for a long time."

"I know, but I had my reasons."

"Well, what are they? And they'd better be good ones."

Hunter shook his head. Ava could be a pain in the butt sometimes. "They're none of your business."

Ava looked affronted. "How are you not going to tell me?"

"Ava, let it go." He knew she recognized that his tone meant the conversation was over when she clamped her jaws shut. He checked the time. "I need to get going, and don't look at me like that. I'll be back, probably sooner than you think, because I have to meet with the hospital board."

"All I know is you'd better not roll up to in here again without saying anything to anybody." She called the children to come say goodbye. Owen had gone to work.

He chuckled and pushed to his feet. After a round of hugs and one more promise to return, he drove to the airport.

As a frequent flyer, he had signed up for the TSA pre-check program when it first rolled out years ago. Little did he know how much it would come in handy now. Having to damn near unpack and undress took more energy than Hunter had to spare these days and he was glad to be able to skip it. The other thing he learned—and continued to have trouble accepting—was that he had to let his pride take a backseat and request a wheelchair to get to and from the gate. When he'd flown in last month, he nearly missed his connecting flight because of the extra time it had taken him to get to the gate. However, this time, the process went effortlessly.

After the long flight to California, he was glad Mark had been adamant about picking him up. Hunter didn't have the strength to drive home.

"Welcome back," Mark said as he smoothly pulled away from the curb. He had flown in for the funeral, but only stayed one night because one of them had to be in the office today. "How did it go with the family?"

"It went. I'm glad it's over. After seeing my Mom and Ava cry, I think I'd do it the same way again."

"Well, at least you don't have to go back for a while."

Hunter scrubbed a hand down his face. "Yeah, I do. In Granddad's will, he asked me to work with an artist to have a mural painted in the new oncology wing he donated."

Mark laughed. "I heard artists can be temperamental. You might have your hands full trying to find one."

"He's already chosen the artist. Michaela."

"Oh, damn."

"Exactly. I already talked to her about it briefly. You can imagine how it went, but I'll tell you about it later." Thankfully, due to the late hour, the drive from LAX to his home in Marina Del Rey only took twenty minutes.

"You coming in tomorrow?" Mark asked as he turned into Hunter's driveway.

"Just for the staff meeting in the afternoon. I may drive by the site in Santa Monica to see how the building is coming along." Hunter grabbed his bag from the back seat. "I appreciate the ride."

"No problem. Later."

He threw up a wave and slowly made his way up the walkway. The long flight had taken a toll on him and all he wanted was his bed. In the past, Hunter would've been at the office by seven, conducted several meetings, gone to the various buildings owned by Prescott Holdings, then come back to the office and not leave until well after eight or nine. These days he felt grateful to be able to walk into the office at all. And he only stayed long enough to take care of whatever task was necessary before heading back home.

After taking a quick shower, he checked his messages. Michaela still hadn't called. He placed it on the charger, but to keep his family from worrying, he decided to send them group text with one word: *Home*. He'd never thought about contacting them whenever he flew back and forth, but he planned to make an effort to stay in better contact with them. He owed them that much. He replaced the phone and climbed into bed.

Thoughts of Michaela filled Hunter's mind as he went to sleep and she was still there the next morning. Once he began to regain his strength, he'd wondered what would happen when he saw her again. He had effectively killed any chance of them being together, but he hoped, one day, she'd understand that he had made that difficult choice because of his love for her.

The fatigue kept him in bed for the better part of the morning, but he felt much better by the time he got to the office. He'd never been one to hold a long meeting and his employees appreciated not having to spend more than an hour, tops. Today, he finished in less time. Hunter went back to his office to pick up a file and Mark followed.

Dropping down into one of the chairs across from Hunter's desk, Mark said, "You were going to tell me what happened with Michaela."

"You're as bad as Ava."

"Hey, I've been keeping this a secret from your family for an entire year, man. And with your scary ass brothers, that should at least get me a few details," he added with a little laugh.

He had to agree about his brothers. They were all different in temperament, but when it came to family, to mess with one meant an automatic ass-whipping. As the Marketing Manager and second in command, Mark had kept the department running when Hunter couldn't. They'd been friends since freshman year of college and Mark's keen knowledge of marketing and advertising made it a no-brainer to bring him on after graduation. "I went to Michaela's place on Sunday to tell her about Granddad's will. She was about as warm as a blizzard, but I expected that. She said she'd think about it and get back to me. So far, she hasn't. But she is still pretty angry." He shared what Michaela had said to him on his way out.

"Did you stay to talk to her about what happened? She's gotta be wondering why you left the way you did. Hell, I don't even know, and I've asked for over a year."

"We didn't discuss it. But we'll have to at some point." Just like he told his sister, only one person deserved those answers. And he had yet to figure out a way to explain it to her.

Friday afternoon, Michaela sat in her office tying up loose ends on several loan documents. Today would be her last day in the office for six weeks and she was looking forward to the time away. After her wedding disaster, she'd thrown herself into the job and had been working non-stop. But she recognized that she had to slow down before she burned out. She had a conference in California for the most of next week, then her vacation would officially begin on Friday. Michaela planned to extend her stay through the weekend to take in some of the sights.

The decision to accept Mr. Prescott's offer to paint the

mural also weighed heavily on her mind. She still hadn't gotten up the nerve to open the envelope or call Hunter. Hunter. If she could stop thinking about him, her life would be so much better. Her sleep patterns had been messed up all week, she had difficulty concentrating on her painting and her nerves were stretched thin.

Michaela completed the last file, locked her desk and almost skipped out of the bank. She pulled her jacket tighter to ward off the chill. The temperatures had dipped into the upper fifties and she looked forward to the near eighty degree weather forecasted for Southern California next week.

Her phone rang as she drove home and she connected the Bluetooth to answer.

"Hey, girl," Lana said in response to Michaela's greeting. "We're still on for tonight, right?"

"Yes. I'm on the way home now." Her two friends were bringing dinner over to celebrate the start of her vacation.

"Okay. We'll see you around seven."

"Sounds good." That would give her a little time start at least one load of laundry.

Once home, Michaela went into cleaning mode and had just removed her clothes from the dryer when her friends arrived.

After filling their plates with the chicken fettucine alfredo and garlic bread, they sat around the dining room table eating for a few minutes. *Three, two, one.*

"Did you get a chance to see Hunter and is he still here?" Melanie asked.

Just like clockwork. "He came by Sunday morning."

Lana and Melanie froze. "*What?*" they chorused.

Lana pointed her fork at Michaela. "That was almost a week ago and you're just now telling us?"

"It was hard seeing him," Michaela admitted. "Harder than

I thought it would be." She placed he fork on her plate. "You remember the new hospital wing Mr. Prescott donated?"

Both women nodded.

"Well, apparently, in his will, he left instructions that a mural be commissioned. He wants me to do it."

"*Ohmigod*," Melanie said with excitement. "Do you know how much that would propel your art career?"

"I don't have an art career."

"My point exactly. How much is he paying you?"

Michaela blinked. She hadn't even asked or considered being paid. She figured she'd be donating her time. "I have no idea. I didn't ask." She forked up some pasta.

Lana snorted. "That would have been the *first* thing I asked. When do you start?"

"I haven't agreed yet."

"What do you mean you haven't agreed to do it? You've been itching to get into the art field for years, and now that you have the opportunity, you're getting cold feet."

"I'm not getting cold feet, Mel. The commission comes with a big catch. I have to work with Hunter."

"Ain't that about a—" Lana cut herself off when Michaela frowned. "Yeah, I know, I know. I'm trying to do better. But I've been cussing more years than not, so it's going to take a minute for me to get used to a cleaner mouth."

She had to smile. Lana could curse a person out in a heartbeat, but she'd been making a concerted effort to cut it down because she didn't want her two young nieces to pick up on her bad habit. But Michaela couldn't be too hard on her friend in this instance, because she'd said more than a few curse words herself in the last week. "Him having to oversee the project means I'll have to see him until it's completed, and I still don't want to talk to him."

"I hope he gave you some reason why he bailed," Melanie

said. "I always thought you two were perfect for each other and, although I can't blame you for being angry, I can tell that you still care about Hunter."

"We didn't talk about that. He said we'd talk about us another time. But I had to remind him there was no us." There would never be an *us* again. She couldn't put herself through the same heartbreak twice, and definitely not with the same man, even if she did still had some lingering feelings deep down inside. They continued eating.

"This damn conversation is too much. I need wine instead of this lemonade." Lana got up from the table and went to the kitchen.

"There's a bottle already in the fridge. Bring me a glass, too," she added.

Melanie laughed. "It's a good thing I brought dessert, too —butter cookies." She wiggled her eyebrows.

"Bless you." The butter cookies from the bakery came in at a close second to the blueberry muffins. Thinking about the muffins reminded Michaela that she needed to pick up a couple to take with her to LA.

Lana came back with the bottle and three wine glasses. She filled them and they finished the meal.

Later, they sat around eating cookies and laughing. "Oh, I forgot to mention that Mr. Prescott left me a letter," Michaela said, sitting up straight.

"Oh, you forgot, my ass." Lana rolled her eyes. "You've been the queen of secrets lately."

"For somebody who's supposed to be cleaning up her potty mouth, you're doing a piss poor job."

"Don't worry about my mouth. Just tell us what the da—. What the letter says."

"I haven't opened it."

Melanie groaned. "Girl, you are killing me. Where is it?"

She pointed to the envelope still lying in the same spot on the table where she'd left it on Sunday.

Melanie picked it up. "I'll read it for you."

She plucked it out of her hand. "I don't think so. I'll do it." Michaela placed her wine glass on the table, took a deep breath and removed the sheet of paper. She read silently.

"Girl, what does it say?" Lana leaned over, trying to see.

"It says that the place needs a facelift and he knows I'm the perfect person to provide it because the painting I'd done for his hospital room brought him such joy and peace. He trusts me to decide what would be best and I'll have free reign to come up with an idea." She decided not to share his reasoning for placing Hunter in charge—Hunter would ensure certain members of the board wouldn't harass her—or the P.S. that said Hunter was the one for her.

"That is so wonderful. You have to do this, Michaela," Lana said.

"I know." Michaela sighed. "I can't let him down."

They shared a group hug and Melanie said, "I'm so proud of you and I have no doubt it will be beautiful."

She nodded. The art she could do. The phone call to Hunter and him playing guardian angel...not so much.

"Well, we'd better get going so you can pack for your vacation." Lana pouted. "I wish I was the one going to sunny California."

"And the weather is going to be so nice for it being the first part of February...eighty degrees, the hotel is near the beach...heaven."

"I so hate you right now."

Laughing, she hugged Lana. "We'll plan a girls trip next time."

Melanie waved a dismissive hand. "Mmm hmm, whatever. You're going to forget all about us when you become this world-renowned artist."

"Girl, please. That won't ever happen. Y'all are my ride-or-die sisters." Michaela saw her friends to the door. "Thank you so much for dinner and the cookies."

"We'll be here on Sunday to drive you to the airport," Lana said. "Don't forget to text us the flight info."

"I won't." After another round of hugs they said their goodbyes.

Michaela came back to the table and reread the letter. That Mr. Prescott trusted her with such a large project without ever seeing much of her work, spoke volumes. And if she had to work with Hunter to get it done, she would grit her teeth, put on her big girl panties and work it like she owned it. She reached for her cell phone and scrolled to the number she hadn't been able to bring herself to delete and before she could lose her nerve, hit the call button. She closed her eyes. *Please let me get his voicemail,* she chanted over and over.

"Hey, Michaela."

Her eyes popped open when she heard Hunter's deep voice. The same voice that used to calm her whenever she became upset, the one that whispered sensuous words in her ear and could turn her on in an instant. The voice that used to say, *I love you.* On second thought, maybe she couldn't do this.

"Michaela?"

"I'm here. Just calling to let you know I'll paint the mural."

"Thank you," Hunter said softly. "Granddad would be happy."

"So, what's next?"

"You and I will meet to talk more in detail, then schedule a time for us to meet with the board and you can take a tour of the place to get a feel for what you might like to do."

"Alright." She hoped he would busy for the next couple of

weeks because she needed a little more time before having to face him again.

"I'd like to get the ball rolling as soon as possible and meet next week."

"Unfortunately, I won't be able to meet next week. I'll be at a banker's conference." Michaela was grateful for the slight reprieve.

"Where's the conference located?"

"In LA. Santa Monica, to be exact." *And far, far away from you.*

"Even better. You'll only be about four or five miles from me."

Aw, shit! She clapped a hand over her mouth, even though she hadn't said the words out loud. Lana was definitely rubbing off on her. "Oh. Are you there for business?"

There was a slight pause, then he said, "I live here."

Michaela knew she shouldn't ask, but she had to know. "How long have you been there?"

"I've been here the entire time."

"I see," she said tightly.

"You don't. Not yet anyway. I'll call you mid-week and we can set up a time to meet. Will that work?"

"Fine."

"Have a safe trip and be careful."

"I will." She tossed the phone on the table. *I hope I'm not making a mistake.*

CHAPTER 3

*M*ichaela all but sprinted out of the hotel's meeting room Thursday afternoon. The last presenter had kept them almost twenty minutes past the four-thirty ending time. She strode down the hall toward the bank of elevators, glad that she'd been able to secure a room at the conference hotel. A few people she'd spoken to had waited too late and were unable to take advantage of the convenience. When the car came, she boarded with the group of people standing there and got off on her floor. Her room, a suite, had a separate living room and a small balcony that provided a distant view of the ocean.

After changing out of her business attire and into a V-neck tee, a pair of crop pants and her sandals, she struck out for a short walk. Santa Monica had a variety of restaurants and shops and her hotel happened to be right in the thick of things, being located near the mall and only a few blocks from the pier. Michaela gravitated to the mall and ended up purchasing a black halter sheath dress, with matching shoes and purse. There was always some bank function or charity event at home and the outfit would work perfectly. On the way out, she stopped by The Cheesecake Factory for Thai lettuce wraps.

Michaela enjoyed her food while sitting on the balcony. For the first time in a long while, she felt herself mentally and physically relax. Even as the evening breeze kicked up and the weather turned cooler, she didn't want to go inside and disturb the small slice of peace she'd found. Her phone rang, shattering her reverie. She picked it up and saw Hunter's name on the display. *There goes my peace.* "Hello."

"Hey. How's the conference going?"

She didn't want him to be nice to her. She wanted him to continue acting like an ass, so she could hate him to her heart's content. "Boring, but what conference isn't?"

Hunter's soft chuckle came through the line. "When I find one, I'll let you know. What time does it end tomorrow?"

It was on the tip of her tongue to lie and say it went until five, but she could hear her mother's lecture about telling the truth in her head. "It ended today."

"Then I'll pick you up tomorrow at six. We can have dinner and talk."

Dinner? "I thought we'd just meet in the lobby or something for a few minutes."

"You do plan to eat dinner tomorrow, correct?"

"Of course." Michaela just didn't want to eat with him and recreate an intimacy that she'd rather not have. In the past, she wouldn't have hesitated. More than likely, she would have suggested they have breakfast, lunch and dinner together, then end the night between silken sheets. Now, she wanted to get in, get the details, and get out. Quick.

"It's only dinner, Michaela. Nothing more. I know of a place in Santa Monica, and if at any time you want to leave, we can."

Stop. Being. So. Nice. She wanted to scream at him. Taking measured breaths, she focused on the fading sunlight and thought about his offer. She did have to eat, she reasoned. "Okay. I'll meet you in the lobby at six." The gentleman in him would want to pick her up and bring her back to her room, but she didn't want him anywhere near her room. "See you tomorrow." She ended the call without waiting for his reply. "I'm doing this for Mr. Prescott," Michaela had to keep reminding herself.

She stayed outside until the cold forced her inside. After channel surfing and not finding anything, she took out her coloring book and colored pencils. Her preference would have been painting, but she hadn't felt like lugging all her supplies across the country and paying the extra baggage fees.

Michaela must have fallen asleep while coloring because when she woke up, she still had a pencil hanging from her hand and she was fully dressed. She struggled to a sitting position and glanced over at the clock. Rubbing her eyes, she checked the time again. "That can't be right," she mumbled. She picked up her phone and gasped. She'd slept until eleven o'clock the next morning. It dawned her that she didn't have anywhere to be, so she laid there a while longer. Admittedly, she felt more rested. A low rumbling began in her belly. What she wouldn't do for a blueberry muffin. But she'd eaten them the first two days in LA.

Not wanting to go out somewhere for food, she got up and searched for the room service menu. After finding it and making her selections, she called it in, then headed for the shower. The food was delivered a few minutes after she finished. Michaela had taken to eating on the balcony every day and carried the tray out to the small table. If she had this view at home, she'd never get anything done because she'd sit here for long periods at a time thinking.

The hours seemed to fly by and the closer it got to the time Hunter was scheduled to pick her up, the more nervous she became. She hadn't even asked him for the type of restaurant. But she knew him and figured it wouldn't be the casual jeans and T-shirt spot. Thankfully, she'd brought a couple extra outfits just in case and chose the black pantsuit with her cream colored camisole. She let her hair hang straight around her shoulders and applied eye liner and lipstick. Taking one last look in the mirror, she stuck her room key in her purse and headed downstairs.

Michaela saw Hunter the moment she stepped off the elevator. He stood at her approach and she noticed he didn't have the cane. And he was wearing all black. One of her most favorite colors on him, not that he didn't look good in anything he wore. With his towering height, smooth dark caramel skin, hair cut low, beard the same, and downright fine self, more than a few women had turned to check him out. And she was no exception. The man had always, always been temptation personified. She wanted to stomp her feet and demand he turn himself into a frog covered in warts.

"You look beautiful."

"Thanks. No cane?"

"It's in the car." Hunter placed his hand in the small of Michaela's back and led her out to the silver Audi parked in front of the door. "I need to go back to my place to pick up the folder first. Something came up at the office and I had to go in, but I didn't want to be late picking you up."

"That's fine." She never had to worry about him being late to anything because he believed in being on time. She'd also wondered about where he had been staying, so in her mind, they'd be killing two birds with one stone, as the saying went. When he mentioned her being only a few miles from him, he meant it. The upscale neighborhood boasted of stately homes on a slight hill with magnificent views of the ocean. *So, this is where you've been hiding.* The beautiful stone design of his two-story home located a block from the ocean captivated her immediately.

He parked in the semi-circular driveway, came around to help her out of the car and escorted her through the front door. "I'll be back in a second. Feel free to look around."

Michaela didn't even know where to begin. Walnut floors, a soaring beamed ceiling and exquisite finishes made for a magnificent structure. The living room, dining room and kitchen all had views of the ocean. How long had he lived here and had he been here alone the entire time? He'd said she could look around, however, Michaela was afraid she'd find some sign that another woman had lived there. What they'd shared was over, so it shouldn't bother her, but for reasons she refused to examine, it did.

"Ready?"

She spun around. "Yes. Your home is beautiful. And you've lived here the entire time, you said?"

The seconds ticked off before he answered. "Thanks, and yes." Hunter gestured her toward the door.

On the drive back, she didn't say much. She stared out at the passing scenery as her mind raced with all sort of scenarios of why he'd moved all the way to California.

True to his word, the restaurant was only five minutes away from her hotel. Infuse Rhythm Lounge turned out to be a nice place that had a large bar in the rear and strategically placed tables and booths around a decent sized stage. The hostess led them to a center table, not too far from the stage. "They have music here?"

"Most weekends. Tonight, Virtual Soul is playing."

Michaela sincerely hoped he didn't plan to stay. She couldn't deal with sitting so close to him all night. He seated her, standing so close she could feel his body heat, then rounded the table to take his own seat. The hostess handed them menus, took their drink order and departed. Minutes later, a server brought the drinks and they made their dinner selections.

"Well, if it isn't Hunter Prescott. I haven't seen you in ages. How're you doing, man?"

She glanced up to see a handsome coffee-colored man standing next to the table.

Hunter stood and shook the man's hand. "Eric. It has been a while. I'd like for you to meet Michaela Saunders. Michaela, this is Eric Dawson, attorney by day and musician by night."

"It's very nice to meet you, Eric," she said. "Those are both full-time careers and must keep you pretty busy."

He laughed. "You're right. That, along with my beautiful wife and baby daughter, doesn't leave me time for much else, and I'm good with it."

Michaela's heart clenched. She felt Hunter's gaze on her, but refused to acknowledge him. *One more strike against him.* "Congratulations, on both," she said sincerely.

Hunter clapped Eric on the back. "That's great news. Congrats."

"Thanks. I hope you're staying for the show." Eric divided his hopeful gaze between Michaela and Hunter.

"Sure," she said. *Just great.* She was two seconds away from a *damn, damn, damn* moment, but she wasn't Florida Evans and she was *not* having a good time.

"Great. Enjoy your dinner and the show. Hunter, I'll be in touch so we can get together."

Hunter nodded. As soon as Eric disappeared into the crowd, Hunter said, "Sorry about that."

Michaela figured saying "no problem" would be a lie, so she didn't reply. A few minutes later, Eric and his band took the stage and the server returned with the food. The dim lighting, candles on the tables and cozy atmosphere, all conspired to push her closer to the edge. It didn't help that every time she looked Hunter's way, she found him staring intently at her.

"This next song is dedicated to a friend of mine and his beautiful lady. Hunter and Michaela, this one is for you." Eric smiled and launched into a sultry ballad.

She dropped her fork and whipped her head toward the stage. *This cannot be happening.* A few—make that a *lot*—of those curse words Lana always spouted popped into Michaela's mind and nearly flew out of her mouth. She met Hunter's sympathetic gaze. It should've given her some sort of conciliation that he looked just as uncomfortable, but she didn't have time to be concerned about his feelings. Not tonight. She only wanted to find a way out of this mess. Her nerves were stretched so thin, she didn't utter a word the entire ride back to her hotel or when Hunter walked her to her room.

"I'm really sorry about what happened, Michaela," Hunter said as soon as the door shut.

"I know. Let's just talk about the mural." He sighed, but didn't push. She took a seat at the desk chair.

He sat on the small loveseat and opened the folder. "We're scheduled to meet with the hospital board on Tuesday afternoon. I'll fly in on Monday, so if you have any questions before the meeting, we can talk then. I understand there will be—"

"Who is she?" Michaela asked quietly.

His head came up. "What?" he asked with confusion. "She who?"

"The woman you left me for."

Hunter slowly closed the folder. "Michaela, there is no other woman. There's never been another woman. I promise you, sweetheart."

"Don't call me that." She jumped up and rushed toward the bedroom, her heart racing and her breathing shallow.

"Michaela." He followed.

She spun around. "Why did you do it? *Why did you leave me? You said you loved me! But you left me,*" she screamed. She launched herself at him, punching him in the chest over and over. "*Why did you leave me?*" she cried.

Hunter banded his arms around her and lost his balance in the process, tumbling them both backwards onto the bed. He held her as she cried her heart out. "I'm sorry, so sorry, baby."

Now that the dam had broken, she couldn't stop crying for all that should have been, for every broken promise, for losing the love of her life. At length, the tears slowed, then stopped.

"Michaela. I didn't leave you because I wanted to, baby. I left because I didn't have a choice." Still cradling her in his arms, he pushed into a sitting position. "Remember me complaining about being tired all the time and you teasing me about being clumsy because I stumbled a few times? It was more than that."

Michaela slowly lifted her head.

"When I left you that message, I was in a Charleston hospital because I couldn't move. The doctor diagnosed me with an inflammatory muscle disease that eventually took away my ability to do anything for myself."

He seemed serious, but…

"I know it's hard to believe and sounds like I'm trying to run a game on you, but I'm telling you the truth." He shifted her enough to dig his phone out of his pocket. He opened the photos and handed it to her.

She didn't know what she expected to see, but she knew it wasn't pictures of him lying in a hospital bed looking like he'd lost a good seventy or eighty pounds, videos of medical personnel helping him with simple tasks like washing his face or trying to walk. "Why didn't you tell me, Hunter?"

"I had no idea how long I'd be confined to a hospital or if I would ever regain the ability to walk again. I had to have someone there twenty-four-seven to do everything for me, right down to wiping my ass. I couldn't even lift my arms to brush my teeth or wash my own face. You have no idea how it feels to need someone to carry you to the bathroom and I didn't want to put you through that kind of torture."

Michaela handed him the phone and left his lap. She paced in front of him. "How could you make that decision for me?" She leaned down close to his face. "We were supposed to be a team, and this is something we should have decided together."

Hunter stood and gave her a rueful smile. "Remember the conversation we had about your father?"

"That has nothing to do with this."

"It has everything to do with my decision. You see, I loved you enough to let you go, to not make you choose. Never doubt my love for you, Michaela. It's the only thing that kept me going when I wanted to give up." He placed a soft kiss on her forehead. "We can talk about the mural another day." Without another word, and with slow steps he walked out.

She heard the door close seconds later and fell across the bed. His revelation stunned her, his choice infuriated her and his last statement confused her. The tears came again and she didn't think they'd ever stop.

Monday, Hunter unlocked the door to his condo in Rosewood Heights and rolled his suitcase to his bedroom. He'd called his housekeeper to let her know he'd be coming in and she had been gracious enough to go the grocery store and pick up a couple of things for him until he could go himself tomorrow. He'd only be in town for a few days, but he'd gotten used to preparing his own food, rather than eating out, and wanted to continue that practice. By the fresh smell, he could tell she'd also cleaned the place and changed his sheets. He tossed his jacket onto a chair, kicked off his shoes and stretched out on the bed. *I really need for this whole fatigue shit to go away.* He used to fly across the country, sometimes twice in a day, with no problem. Now he'd be lucky not to be exhausted halfway through the first flight. But this time, something more had drained his energy. He'd replayed Michaela's breakdown in his mind so many times, he could almost hear her screams and feel her small fists pounding his chest. His hand involuntarily went to the spot. He had planned to call her over the weekend, but they both needed time. Even if they didn't talk before the meeting tomorrow, he knew she'd do fine. And he would be there to make sure of it. His eyes drifted closed.

The insistent buzzing in his pocket awakened Hunter. He dug it out and sighed. "Hey, Dom."

"You make it in yet?"

"Yep." He sat up. "I'm at my place."

"We'll be there in a minute."

He didn't even have to ask about the "we" in his brother's statement. Running his hand over his head, he swung his legs over the side of the bed and sat there a moment. He sent a text to Ava to let her know he'd made it and to schedule a time to visit sometime on Wednesday, then sent a message to his parents.

As soon as he set the phone down, it buzzed again. Hunter read the text from Dominic saying he had arrived. He punched in the gate code and went to open the door. His brothers filed in and spread out across the living room. "I'm surprised you all are still here."

"I'm not going to be here much longer," Dominic said. He'd made his home in Miami, but traveled extensively.

"I'm out soon, too." Maverick, who lived in Las Vegas, tossed out as he came back from the kitchen grumbling about Hunter not having any food.

Hunter shook his head. "I just got here, Mav, so if you wanted food, then you should've stopped and brought your own." His smart baby brother not only served as Chief Financial Officer for the family business, but also owned a night club. "Cooper?" Hunter said when his twin sat silently. "I figured you'd be back in Detroit running your construction company by now."

"Yeah, me, too. But I might be here a little while longer and don't y'all say shit."

"Hmm, interesting." Although he maintained a seat on the board, Cooper was the only brother not actively involved in the day-to-day operations of Prescott Holdings, something their father had never been happy about.

"What's interesting is that bullshit explanation you gave at the house. I know there's more to it and I'm not leaving until I get answers."

Hunter should've known Dominic would see straight through the watered down version of his illness. At six-four, Dominic eclipsed Hunter's height by two inches, and was built like an NFL linebacker, which made him perfect in his role of Chief Security Officer at Prescott Holdings. And he took his big brother role a little too serious at times. Like now. Instead of saying anything, he opened the photos, and just like he'd done with Michaela, passed him the phone.

Maverick scooted closer to look, as well.

He shared a look with Cooper, who had seen the pictures when he visited. Both Maverick and Dominic alternated between shakes of their heads and a softly muttered, "damn."

"Does Michaela know?" Maverick asked as he passed the phone back. "I don't even know how you walked away from her."

"Yeah. I told her when she came to LA last week. And I didn't walk away from her because I wanted to, smart ass." He shared how she'd broken down and their conversation about why he'd made that particular choice.

Dominic shook his head. "That still doesn't make sense, Hunter. She should've been with you."

"You still love her?" Cooper asked.

"Never stopped. What I went through would test the strongest person, and like I said, I couldn't put her through that, not knowing whether I'd recover and to what extent. There's more, but it's something she and I have to work out." He hoped it would be soon because fatigue and sleepless nights did not go well together. "Now, if this damn inquisition is over, can y'all take your asses home so I can sleep? I'm tired as hell."

"Why didn't you say something?" Dominic asked.

Hunter snorted. "Like you would've listened."

He laughed as he came to his feet. "You're right. I wouldn't have." He turned serious. "If you need anything, let one of us know. Well, maybe except Cooper, since he doesn't tell anybody's shit."

Cooper glared. "Shut the hell up, Dom. Aren't we leaving?"

Hunter just shook his head. It was never a dull moment with the Prescott clan.

After they finally left, Hunter thought about tomorrow's meeting. He toyed with sending Michaela a text to see if she had any questions or concerns, but decided against it. Instead he headed for the shower, then bed.

He woke up Tuesday morning feeling better. He'd been trying to ditch the cane, but the weakness showed up randomly and other than going short distances, he still didn't trust that his body wouldn't betray him.

Hunter mentally went over how he planned to handle

things if Tom McFarland proved to be difficult. He didn't know the man well, but had heard that he enjoyed throwing his weight around and thought more highly of himself than he should due to his position on the board. He also knew from Granddad's letter that Tom wanted his daughter to do the mural and would try to get the board to reverse its decision. But he'd done a little research on his own and found out a few interesting pieces of information that he would share, if necessary. The man might be used to getting his way, but today, it wouldn't be happening. And if he directed one negative comment toward Michaela, Hunter would rip him to shreds.

With his game plan firmly set, he met up with Cooper for a late breakfast.

"Are you sure you're good, bruh?" Cooper asked.

"Yeah, but having to take naps like I'm a damn two-year old has gotten really old."

"And Michaela? I know you said you still love her, but do you think the two of you will get back together?"

"I honestly don't know." Hunter placed his fork on his plate. "We still have to clear the air about the way I left and why first. Enough about me. What's going on that you're still here? Is Dad still hassling you about joining the company?"

"You know he's probably never going to let that shit go, but right now, I'm just working on what Granddad asked me to do with restoring a house. After that, we'll see."

"Do what makes you happy, Coop." All the brothers had been supportive of his choice not to work for the company and make his own mark, and they would continue to have Cooper's back.

"As soon as you do it your damn self," Cooper threw out without looking up from cutting his pancakes.

Laughing, he could only nod. Having Michaela back in his life would make him happy, but he hadn't seen or felt happy in over a year, and didn't think that would change any time soon.

They continued eating, then Cooper asked, "How long are you staying?"

"At least a couple more days. Michaela and I are meeting with the hospital board this afternoon about the mural Granddad wants painted in the new wing."

Cooper chuckled.

"What?"

"You have to work with the woman you ghosted—and who probably hates your guts—for the next however many weeks. That's some cold shit."

"Yeah." On some level Hunter agreed with his brother. Michaela still didn't get that he'd done it for her because he knew how she felt about certain things. He didn't know if she would ever understand. If she didn't, he'd lose her for good. They finished their meal and went their separate ways.

Later, Hunter arrived ten minutes before the scheduled three o'clock meeting. He made a mental note to ask Michaela about her work schedule and whether she planned to take off while painting or fit it into her schedule. The latter would mean the project could take much longer. He saw Michaela enter the building and stood. His gaze made a lingering path down her body and back up. The red skirt suit molded to her curves and his hands itched to caress them. After holding her in his arms last week, he wanted nothing more than to do it all over again. This time minus the tears.

"Hunter," Michaela said by way of greeting.

"How are you?"

"Okay."

He noticed she would barely look at him and opened his mouth to tell her that everything would be alright, but stopped when he saw two of the board members.

"Thank you so much for coming," one of the members

said. "We know your time is valuable, so we'll get started. Follow me."

He and Michaela followed behind the woman. As soon as they got to the door, Hunter paused and whispered, "You're going to do just fine, and I'll be there to make sure everything goes as it should."

"Thank you." She gave him a trembling smile.

Inside, after a round of introductions, they got down to business. Two minutes in, Tom started.

"I think we should give careful consideration to finding someone with more experience," Tom said. "Or at least have someone assist and supervise."

The board's chairperson sighed. "Tom, we've been over this before. When Mr. Prescott donated the wing, the stipulations included his choice of persons to create the mural. He's chosen Ms. Saunders, and we will govern ourselves accordingly."

"My daughter has far more experience and has been painting much longer than Ms. Saunders."

Hunter saw the fire leap in Michaela's eyes. He gave her hand a reassuring squeeze.

"She's done a commissioned painting for—"

"How many paintings has your daughter sold, Mr. McFarland?" Hunter asked.

Silence.

"I take that to mean she hasn't sold one. Ms. Saunders, on the other hand has sold at least a dozen, has had showings at prominent art festivals and was commissioned to do the artwork for a local doctor's office. But that's neither here nor there." He leaned forward. "My grandfather's last wishes state that *she* is to complete the mural and the board has voted in the affirmative. It would be a shame for the funding to be pulled at such a late date if we can't come to an agreement."

Tom visibly blanched.

"That won't be necessary, Mr. Prescott," the chairperson rushed to say.

That's what I thought. Hunter shifted his gaze to Michaela and found her viewing him strangely. He'd give anything to know what she was thinking.

$\mathcal{M}$ichaela marveled at the way Hunter had handled Mr. McFarland. No better way to get that old fart's attention than to threaten to withhold money. He hadn't raised his voice, but the quiet authority had crackled across the room like a whip. It reminded her of the first day they'd met at a Charleston art festival three years ago. She'd been arguing with a potential customer who had been trying to haggle down the price of one of her paintings. Hunter had pointedly told the man they weren't at the flea market, and if he wasn't going to purchase the painting to step aside. When the man had balked, Hunter whipped out his wallet, slapped down his credit card and purchased it for himself. The wink and smile he'd shot her afterwards had gone straight to her heart and she'd fallen in love with him that instant. Every moment thereafter had been like something out of a fairy tale. Until it fell apart. *I didn't want to put you through that.* Michaela had been trying to understand why ever since. One of the board members talking filtered into her thoughts.

"If you're ready, we can tour the space where you'll be working, Ms. Saunders."

"That would be great." Before she could move, Hunter was already on his feet and helping her up.

Hunter smiled. "You good, baby?" he whispered.

"Yes. Thank you." How could she not be okay with him as her champion? As if nothing had ever separated them, he entwined their fingers, sending both awareness and confusion flowing through her. The part of her that knew things weren't settled between them wanted to pull away. However, a small part inside of her—the part that had missed him—wanted his touch. Still craved it.

The group entered a new building that still smelled of fresh paint. The stark white walls were primed and awaiting her inspiration. Once again, Michaela's emotions swelled. The opportunity that she'd been granted was something she would always be grateful for and she vowed to make Mr. Prescott proud. There were two wings, one for adults and another for children. An idea came to her. "Would it be possible to paint a mural on each side? Both would inspire calmness and peace, but I'd like to do something a little different for the children that reflects their carefree spirits."

"The agreement is—," Mr. McFarland began.

"The agreement is for Ms. Saunders to do the mural. Period." The quelling look Hunter shot the man made him clamp his jaws shut and turn away in a huff.

Michaela wanted to cheer. *Ha! Take that, you old goat!*

"Oh, that's a wonderful idea," one woman said. "I can already see it." She clasped her hands together against her chest. "The center is scheduled to open mid-March. Do you think you can have it done by then?"

She did a mental calculation in her head. With her being on vacation, she could devote all her time to the murals. "Yes." It dawned on her that she had no idea about supplies.

Did the hospital expect her to purchase them? She'd have to ask Hunter about it later. "Will I be limited to certain hours?"

"We'll have security patrolling this area from seven to six and we'd like to confine your time to anytime within that timeframe," Mr. McFarland said. "Will that be a problem?"

"Not at all. I would like to have the area covered until it's completed." Michaela wanted the finished work to be a surprise. She could hardly contain her excitement and couldn't wait to celebrate with Lana and Melanie. A soft nudge from Hunter brought her back into the conversation where the chairperson was asking if she had any questions. Once again, she'd been caught daydreaming. "No, I don't have any questions at the moment. I'd just like to say that I'm honored to be given this opportunity and I don't take it lightly. I will be forever grateful to Mr. Prescott and you and will do my best to create a warm environment that'll provide comfort for families going through difficult times with their loved ones." *You see, I loved you enough to let you go, to not make you choose. Never doubt my love for you, Michaela. It's the only thing that kept me going when I wanted to give up.* Her breath caught. Hunter had gone through those times alone, when she should've been there. *But he took that option away from you,* a sage inner voice reminded her. As they all left the building and went their separate ways, Hunter stopped her.

"You zoned out back there for a minute. Is everything okay?" he asked, critically studying her.

"Oh. Yeah. I was just thinking about some ideas," she lied. "Do you know if I'll need to purchase my own paint and supplies?"

"No. I'll take care of everything. All I need is for you to let me know the cost. I've been meaning to ask you about your job. Will you be taking time off or working around your bank schedule?"

Michaela nodded. "Okay. And I'll be on vacation for the

next several weeks, so I'll be able to devote all my time to the mural. Um...I know you probably have things to do, so I'll see you later." She pivoted on her heel and hurried across the lot to her car. Her plan had been to call her friends, but she needed to talk to the one person who could, hopefully, make sense of what Michaela was feeling.

She parked in front of her mother's house, got out and let herself in. "Mom," she called out as she walked through the foyer.

"Michaela." Her mother rounded the corner with her arms outstretched and a big smile.

She fell into her mother's arms and held on. These were the arms that had comforted her when she skinned her knee after trying to do a somersault in the driveway. When she lost the spelling bee in eighth grade. When she missed being valedictorian by less than one-tenth of a percent. When she'd endured the whispers and stares after being a jilted bride. This was the solace she needed and it took all her effort not to break down.

Her mother eased back and ran a loving hand over Michaela's cheek. "I'm in the kitchen getting ready to make a pan of cornbread to go with the pot of chili," she said as she started in that direction. "You're welcome to stay for dinner. How was the conference?"

"Boring for the most part, but there were a couple of gold nuggets. Mmm, that smells so good," Michaela said as she lifted the lid and inhaled the smoky concoction. Rochelle Saunders made the best chili on the planet in her estimation.

"What's going on, sweetheart?"

She slowly rotated and met her mother's concerned gaze. *How does she do that?* "Is it that obvious?"

"Only to someone who knows you well," she said and gestured toward a chair.

"Can I ask you a question?" Michaela sat and her mom took the chair next to her.

"Sure."

"When Dad was sick, why didn't you hire someone to come in and take care of him or have him transferred to a nursing home during those last few months?" She recalled how exhausted her mother always was and the many nights she cried. There had been an aide who came one or two days a week for a few hours while her mother ran her various errands, but other than that, Rochelle had shouldered the burden alone.

"I loved him. When I married Brian Saunders, I promised to love him through sickness and health and I took those vows seriously. That's what love is all about, honey, and I couldn't leave that to some stranger who didn't know him or care. I wanted him to know that no matter what, I'd be there for him, doing whatever was necessary to make sure he didn't face those long, hard days alone."

Michaela studied her hands. "I saw Hunter."

"Yes, at the funeral. I did, too. I was worried because he looks a little unwell and like he's lost some weight."

Unwell didn't begin to define what he'd gone through.

"I also noticed that he couldn't keep his eyes off you. It's very apparent that he still loves you."

Her head came up. She knew he did, and he'd said as much last week.

"But what does this have to do with your father?"

"Mr. Prescott donated the new cancer wing at the hospital and he commissioned me to do a mural for it."

"Oh, Michaela, that's wonderful. I hope this will be just the thing to open the door to you starting your art career. You've been talking about it for a long time."

"But he left Hunter in charge of overseeing the project."

Her mother leaned back in the chair. "Oh. And how do you feel about that?"

"Loaded question, Mom. I'm so mixed up right now, I don't know if I'm coming or going. He lives in LA and we were supposed to meet and discuss the project, but ended up having a major blow up. Let me rephrase that—*I* had a major blow up or meltdown, or whatever you want to call it. He was in the hospital for months and he never told me." Tears welled up in her eyes. "He said he loved me and didn't want to put me through the torture."

"That had to be so hard for him, but I don't understand why he just didn't come right out and say it."

"His family didn't even know. He mentioned some old conversation we'd had about Dad and told me it was because he didn't want me to have to choose."

"I see," her mother said softly.

"That makes one of us."

"Do you remember how adamant you were about wanting me to hire someone to come in to care for your father or letting him stay in the hospital?"

Michaela frowned. "Yes, but that had nothing to do with Hunter. He *left me*, Mom," she said, the tears starting to flow.

"Baby, it has everything to do with him and the decision he made," she said, covering Michaela's hand. "Hunter loved you enough not to force you to make the same choice that I did. Actually, I'd venture to say he was more afraid of what choice you'd make."

The weight of her mother's words slammed into her like a freight train and she found it hard to breathe. *No way could I do what my mom did with my father and be that exhausted every day, all day. I'd definitely have to hire someone to come in and help.* Along with the memory of what she'd told him, images all of the photos and videos Hunter had shown her rushed back, nearly overwhelming her. "No, no, no," she whispered, clutching her chest. "*Ohmigod,* Mom." Michaela brought one hand to her mouth and wrapped the other around her midsection as a sob broke free. She dropped her head to her knees. "He was right." The guilt surged up and nearly drowned her. Hunter had remembered that one small conversation and knowing she would do exactly as she'd told him, had given her an out. To not make her have to choose between living up to the vows she had planned to speak and watching him suffer for who knew how long. He loved her enough to make the ultimate sacrifice of letting her go, but would she have loved him enough to hang in there with him? Michaela didn't want to look into the shadowy corner of her heart that might give her an answer she didn't like. Hunter had been afraid she wouldn't choose him. The knowledge that she'd put that fear in his heart made the tears come faster.

"It's going to be okay, baby," her mother said, her arms wrapped firmly around her.

"It's not going to be okay, Mom. It's not ever going to be okay because I messed up. I made him think I wouldn't be there for him and love him like you loved Dad. I did that." She'd been so angry about what *he'd* done, and even after their last conversation, she still wanted to place all the blame on him. But this was on her. Her father had always told her to weigh her words carefully because they had power. Her words had power, all right, and they destroyed the most precious love she'd ever known.

"Michaela, look at me."

It took a lot of effort to raise her head, as the shame of her words continued to bombard her.

"I can't say whether or not you would've left his care to someone else, but I know you love Hunter and he loves you, and that's a good place to begin. You're not that same twenty-something woman you were when your father died.

I've watched you grow into a thirty-three year-old woman who goes after what she wants. The question is do you love Hunter enough to fight for him?"

"I do."

A soft smile curved her lips. "Then what you need to do is put on your big-girl panties and go after him. Maybe this time I *will* get to hear those two little words," she added with a chuckle.

Two little words? Michaela viewed her mother curiously. Then it dawned her. *I do.* She hugged her mother. "I love you, Mom." And as soon as she got home, she was finding those big-girl panties.

Saturday morning, Hunter and Mark worked out in Hunter's home gym. More like Mark worked out and Hunter did something that resembled a kindergartner learning how to exercise for the first time. He should be grateful, however, because he could actually use dumbbells—he'd finally graduated from single digit weights—and a couple of the machines.

"Have you talked to Michaela since the meeting?" Mark asked.

He stared enviously at his friend bench-pressing two-hundred and forty-five pounds like it weighed only ten. "No. I'm not sure how to approach her after what happened when she was here last week."

Mark sat up. "What happened last week?"

Hunter had forgotten that he and Mark hadn't talked outside of business and Hunter had flown home right after the weekend. "Everything finally came to a head and I told her what happened and why I left."

He used a towel to wipe the sweat from his face. "Now that the cat is out of the bag, care to enlighten me?"

"When we first started dating three years ago, we were talking about her father dying from cancer and how her mother had taken care of him. She said something to the effect that she would've paid someone to come in and take of him or send him to a nursing home because of how exhausted her mother had been all the time. That she wouldn't be able to deal with it." He did the last set of ten on the leg press. "I just made the decision easier for her." Hunter didn't fear many things, but the thought of his wife—the one person he wanted to be able to give him the assurance that he would be okay, even if she didn't believe the words at first—choosing to throw him away in some nursing home had scared the hell out of him. He knew his family would have come in a heart-beat, but Michaela was the only one he wanted. So he'd done things his way—quietly, quickly and without a lot of fuss.

"She was probably just saying that. I mean, would she have really done it, though? Michaela loved you and I can't see her just walking away like that." Mark waved a hand for emphasis.

"You weren't there for the conversation and maybe not, but I couldn't take that chance." Hunter did wonder if he'd done the right thing by showing her the photos or telling her all the details, but he wanted her to understand how difficult it would have been for her. His mind went back to those dark times, and he whispered a prayer of thanks for how far he'd come. He now appreciated the small things like being able to brush his own teeth. The doorbell rang.

"You expecting someone?"

"No," Hunter said, carefully pushing to his feet. He stood there a couple of seconds to make sure his legs were steady and left to answer the door. *Michaela.* He snatched it open.

"Michaela, hey. What are you doing here?" He glanced down at the purple carryon, then peered around her to see how she'd gotten there.

"Lyft. May I come in?"

"Yeah." He moved aside for her to enter. "Why didn't you tell me you were coming? I would've picked you up from the airport."

A corner of Michaela's mouth kicked up into a smile. "I didn't decide myself until yesterday."

He was so stunned, he didn't know what to say. "Um, how did you get my address?" They had stopped by for a few minutes when she'd come for her conference, but he hadn't written anything down for her.

"I ran into Cooper and I figured if anyone knew where you were, it would be him. And I was right."

So much for his brother not telling other people's shit.

Mark came into the room. "Michaela. It's been a while. How are you?"

"Hey, Mark. I'm okay."

"Hunter, I'm going to take off. I'll see you on Monday." He bent and kissed Michaela's cheek. "It's really good to see you."

As soon as he closed the door behind him, Michaela said, "I'm sorry. I didn't mean to interrupt."

Hunter eased the luggage from her hand, led her through the foyer to the room he'd set up as a den and gestured her to a seat. "You aren't interrupting anything. Can I get you something?" For some reason, she seemed nervous and it gave him pause.

She shook her head.

Perched on the edge of the sofa, she wrung her hands together. "I probably should've called...I mean, I hope it's okay, me showing up and..."

He lowered himself next to her and grasped both of her

hands. "Michaela, it's no problem. Did something happen with the hospital board or are you having an issue with the mural?"

"No." She bowed her head, as if trying to gather her thoughts. After a lengthy minute she said in a barely audible voice, "You were right."

She lifted her head and misery stared back at him. Hunter's heart started pounding.

"I finally understand what you meant and I'm *so* sorry, Hunter. I should've been there with you and not allowed you to go through all the pain alone. It's my fault that you believed I wouldn't be there and I couldn't have been more selfish."

"Michaela—"

"No. Let me finish, please. I *was* selfish and talking to my mom made me realize just how wrong I'd been." Michaela pulled her hands from his and framed his face. I should have loved you better so that you'd know I wouldn't leave your side for one moment, for any reason. If I had to do it all again, you'd know. I *would* love you better."

Hunter's emotions surged with such force, he couldn't control the tears forming in his eyes. "More than anything, I wanted you there, but I was afraid." He had never admitted his fears out loud, or to anyone. He could always handle whatever life threw his way. Not this time. This time, his man card was about to be torn to shreds.

"Afraid that I'd leave your care to someone else or possibly put you in a nursing home like I had suggested to my mother." She shook her head. "All this time, I thought you didn't want me." Her voice cracked. "That you didn't love me anymore."

"I never, *never*, stopped loving you, not for one minute, not even one second. Letting you go was the hardest thing I've ever had to do. I met some people who are still suffering and showing no signs of improvement. I had no idea if I was going to be one of those people, and I didn't want to sentence you to the same type of hell I had to live in, maybe for a lifetime. If I had to do it all again, I'd make the same choice."

"No, you wouldn't because I'm going to love you better."

Hunter's heart pounded even harder. "Michaela?"

"I want the chance to show you that I can be the woman who won't run at the first sign of trouble, the one who will be there no matter what, the one who will take care of your heart the way you've taken care of mine."

A tear slid down his cheek. *Damn! There goes my man card.* It took all his strength to keep more from falling.

"I love you, Hunter Prescott, and I don't ever want to be without you again."

The tender kiss that followed would have knocked him to his knees if he'd been standing. Hunter hadn't thought about kissing or anything else in over a year, but it didn't take him long to catch up. He pulled her closer, angled his head and slowly, sensually reacquainted himself with the familiar sweetness of her kiss and reminding himself why only Michaela Saunders would ever be the one for him.

CHAPTER 5

*M*ichaela giggled as she read the text from Hunter. She'd been back from her impromptu trip for two weeks and her work on the murals was progressing nicely. They'd talked just about every night, discussed their mistakes, and made promises to always be transparent with each other. The closeness they'd previously shared seemed to be even better this time.

Melanie reached over and snatched the phone. "We did not come to spend our Friday evening watching you send nasty text messages to Hunter. I thought we came to celebrate the start of your art career, which technically, was supposed to happen *two weeks ago* until somebody, who shall remain nameless, up and flew across the country."

She grabbed the phone back. "It was for a good reason."

"I guess so, because your ass hasn't stopped smiling since we got here," Lana said. "And I want to know what happened. Are you and Hunter back together or what?"

"Yep."

Melanie narrowed her gaze. "Okay, color me confused. You hooked back up with the man who pretty much left you at the altar, that had you depressed and hiding out in your house for a good three months, and you're...happy? Who. Does. That?"

Michaela leaned back and closed her eyes. "It wasn't completely his fault."

Lana held up her hands. "Wait, wait, wait. How isn't it his fault? Wasn't he the one who left the voicemail saying 'something came up' and he wasn't going to make it? Sounds like it is *completely* his fault. Ooh, these men will say anything to get back in your good graces. And don't jump back into bed with them because it'll be a wrap and you'll be back exactly where you started." She skewered Michaela with a look. "You didn't give up the goodies, did you?"

"No, I did not, and he hasn't tried to get me into bed. I'm not saying him up and disappearing the way he did isn't his fault. It is. But after talking to him and listening to what he had to say, I realized that I had some responsibility in the way things went down. I'm going to share this, but it better not leave this room." Hunter had always valued his privacy and she doubted he wanted his business spread all over town. With him being one of *The* Prescotts, it would spread faster than a brushfire. Michaela divided her gaze between her friends, waiting for a sign of agreement.

Both nodded and Lana said, "I'll take it to the grave, girl."

"Okay, he has an inflammatory muscle disease and was in the hospital from the time he left the bachelor party until July. I know it sounds like he was full of it, but I saw the pictures of him. It was bad." Every time she thought about how he'd been alone, it made her heart ache. He'd even opened up to her a little about his depression. She wished she could go back in time and slap a hand over her mouth to keep from spouting that foolishness about what she wouldn't do. Now that she had finally gotten her head back on straight, she could very well see his point of view. Had he said something similar to her, she might have made the same choice. "He lost the ability to move and needed someone to help him with everything, and I do mean *everything*. He even had to learn how to walk all over again." Michaela told herself she wasn't going to cry again as she felt the tears stinging her eyes. She'd shed more tears in the past two weeks than she had in eight months.

"Damn. Well, you did say the only excuse you would accept was him being dead or close to it, and I hate to tell you, sis, but this sounds like he was close and you're going to have to give the brother a pass." Lana snapped her fingers. "Oh, so that's why he has the cane."

"That still doesn't explain why it wasn't his fault," Melanie said.

"He left because of something I'd said in passing early in our relationship about not wanting to be like my mother when she took care of my dad." Melanie and Lana knew well how Michaela felt during that time, as she had vented to them often. She shared the details of her conversation with Hunter and how it had impacted his decision. "The thing is, I don't think he would've been wrong back then. All I remember thinking is I didn't want to end up like my mom. That's not the case now."

"I remember you being upset and worried that your mother was going to end up sick because of all the things she had to do to help your father. I can't imagine how hard that had to be, in both cases, but I'm guessing if you say you love someone, you have to take the bad with the good."

"Which is exactly what my mother said to me. She reminded me that love is an action word, and not just an emotion. So, yeah, I am partly to blame."

"Are you guys going to set a new date?" Melanie asked.

"We just started talking again, and it's way too early to bring it up."

"But if he asked you to marry him again, would you do it?"

"In a heartbeat." When she thought she hated Hunter, deep inside, she realized the hate hadn't erased the love and she couldn't imagine spending the rest of her life with anyone other than him. She felt even stronger about her decision now that the animosity had dissipated.

"That's double good news, then. I really am happy for you, Michaela. We always thought you and Hunter belonged together and I hope you two make it this time."

"Thanks, Lana. I hope we do, too." Michaela wouldn't accept anything less.

"We need to toast and get this party started. To the start of Michaela's new career and a stronger love." Melanie cranked up the music and the three woman danced and sang.

Michaela hadn't felt this relaxed and happy in a long time. These two woman had been by her side almost her entire life, sharing in her triumphs and failures. And this moment definitely qualified as the former.

It was well after midnight, when she saw her friends out and fell across her bed and into a deep sleep.

The next morning, Michaela dressed and drove over to the hospital to work on the mural. In hindsight, she should have asked about the weekend hours, but almost squealed when the guard said she could go in. She had decided to start on the children's side first and loved how the scene was coming together. With her music playing in the background and Hunter in her life again, her concentration had skyrocketed and the hours passed in a blur. It took the security guard reminding her that the doors would be locked soon for her to clean up and leave.

Michaela checked the time and realized she had less than fifteen minutes to get to her mother's house for dinner. She glanced down at her paint-splotched clothes and debated whether to go home and change first and be late or go as-is and decided on the latter.

When her mother opened the door, she just shook her head. "My child still loves to play in paint. Come on in."

Laughing, she said, "I thought about going home to change, but I know how you are about being on time for dinner. I had only planned to paint for three or four hours, but lost track of time."

"As always." Her mom pulled a pan of barbeque chicken from the oven. "I made a few extra pieces for you to take home. Now that you're working on that mural, I know you're barely taking time to cook or eat."

Michaela opened her mouth to refute her mother's words, but couldn't, so she closed it. "Thanks, Mom." Growing up, her parents often had to drag her away from a canvas to do her chores, eat, or anything else. Her cell rang and she searched her tote to find it. She smiled when she saw Hunter's name. "Hey, handsome."

"Hey, baby. How's the mural going?"

"Good. I went in today for a few hours and I'm almost done with the children's mural."

Hunter laughed. "A few hours? More like the security guard had to drag your butt out when it was time for the building to close."

"Nobody asked you." She quieted. "I never thought I hear your laugh again."

"I hear you, but I'm glad to have you back in my life again."

"So am I. Are you coming home anytime soon?" Her mind understood that they couldn't make up for lost time, but her heart didn't want him out of her sight again.

"Probably not for another couple of weeks. With the new resort opening soon and renovations being done at one of the casinos, I have to make sure the marketing plans are in place. But I'll definitely be there next month for the unveiling."

Disappointment filled her. "Oh. I was kind of hoping to see you sooner. I would come to you, but I don't want to mess up my flow."

"The time will go by fast. What are you doing?"

She'd completely forgotten that her mother was there listening and hazarded a glance over her shoulder. Her mother stood leaning against the counter with a knowing smile on her face. "I'm having dinner with Mom."

"Tell her I said hello, and I'll be by to talk to her the next time I come home."

"I'll do that. I know she'll love to see you. I'd better go so the food doesn't get cold."

"I love you, Michaela."

"Love you, too." She held the phone against her heart, never tiring of hearing him declare his love.

"I see things are moving pretty quickly with you and Hunter," her mother said, handing Michaela a plate.

"It's almost as if we're picking up where we left off, but different," she said while loading the chicken, mashed potatoes and spinach onto her plate. "Does that even make sense?" The old familiarity had come back, but the connection seemed to be different, deeper.

"It makes perfect sense. This experience has caused you both to grow. Adversity has a way of stretching you like nothing else."

"Ain't that the truth. I'd rather skip it though, and just have a boring predictable, no drama life."

"Wouldn't we all? Michaela, I understand how wonderful this all is, but make sure you're ready to do this relationship for the long haul, that if some other hard challenge comes around, you'll hang in there at all costs. Honey, if you're not ready for that, then you and Hunter are going to be right back where you were last year."

Michaela digested her mother's words. "I get it, Mom. I do admit that I had some fairy tale vision of what marriage should be like, but I know better now. Although, I do believe I'll still have my fairy tale because, yeah, Hunter is totally a prince."

Her mother burst out laughing. "That always helps."

She grinned. "It does, but I'm also realistic enough to realize that life doesn't always play by my rules. I only have to look at what happened to Dad and Hunter to see it. And, Mom, I am truly sorry for the things I said back then. I was concerned about losing both my parents—Dad to cancer and you from exhaustion. But something came to mind yesterday that I, somehow, buried. Although taking care of Dad wore you out and I'd hear you crying at night," she started, then paused at the sound of her mom's soft gasp. Michaela reached for her hand. "I heard you, Mom, even though I know you didn't want me to, that you were trying to be strong for me and for Dad. But I also remember your words of love to him, and hearing you tell him how much you'd been blessed by having him in your life. Those are the things I should've kept in my heart, instead."

"Those are the most important things," she said, giving Michaela's hand a gentle squeeze.

"Yes, they are." Michaela's feelings for Hunter mirrored that of her mother and father. And if, for some reason, he had a relapse, she planned to be right there whispering how much she loved him, telling him how much he'd blessed her life, and assuring him that she'd be right there and it would be okay. That he could always, *always* count on her.

～

"Dinner was great, Mom," Hunter said, wiping his mouth on a cloth napkin. When he'd let his parents know he'd be flying in that Tuesday, his mother had invited him—ordered him would be a better description—to come to dinner. He'd come straight from the airport. Luckily, Ava and her family had joined them, so he had one less visit to make.

"I'm so glad you could carve out a little time out to visit. I know you've been busy getting back into the swing of things at Prescott Holdings and overseeing the mural."

"Hard not to carve out time when you didn't really give me a choice," he drawled.

Ava snickered and shot Hunter a quick look.

His mother smiled sweetly, then asked, "How is Michaela doing on the mural?"

Hunter wasn't stupid. She'd asked the double-edged question to get information about the status of his and Michaela's relationship. "I haven't actually seen it. She mentioned not wanting anyone to see it until it's finished. But I know she's been working long hours on them. She decided to do two—one on the children's side and the other on the adult wing." He deliberately didn't include any personal information about their relationship. Over the past couple of weeks, his conscience had been giving him a beatdown about the way he'd left. He could only imagine all the humiliation Michaela must have endured, and she'd had to do it alone. He owed her a huge apology.

She lifted an eyebrow. "And the two of you?"

Damn, Mom. Some things are meant to be private. He shrugged. "We haven't talked much." *Today.*

"I do hope—"

"Brenda, leave it be," his father said, cutting her off. "If Hunter has something to tell, he will. He's a grown man and can handle his own business."

Hunter sent his dad a grateful look, and deciding he definitely needed to take the spotlight off himself, engaged his niece in a conversation about the new book she'd shown him earlier.

After dinner, Ava hooked her arm in his and steered him off to the side. "I happened to see Michaela at Roseberry Bakery yesterday and she was smiling. A lot."

"And?"

"She hasn't smiled much in the last several months, but all of a sudden, *after* you return from no man's land—which, by the way, I still have no clue where that is—she's walking around with a big ole goofy grin."

"One, I don't live in *no man's land*. Two, you know I've been going back and forth between here and LA for the past four years. And three, did it ever occur to you that Michaela's smile has nothing to do with me and everything to do with being tapped for one of the biggest projects in Rosewood Heights?"

"I'm sure that's part of it, but *trust me*, only a *man* can make a woman walk around with that kind of look on her face. I should know." She wiggled her eyebrows.

Hunter made a face. "That's too much damn information, Ava. I do not want to hear this kind of sh—" He cut himself off when he spotted Little Sully walk into earshot. "*Stuff* from my baby sister."

She waved a dismissive hand. "Oh, please. I've pushed two babies out of my—"

He threw up his hands and stalked off, her laughter following. He did not need her to provide graphic details of having babies. Yes, she was a grown woman and married, but she would always be his baby sister and, as irrational as it seemed, he planned to keep that view of her.

"You been feeling okay, Hunter?" his father asked as Hunter passed.

"I'm doing pretty good. I still get tired if I do too much, though. But I'm on top of things at the office, so no worries."

"Your health is far more important than the job."

Now that's a first. Edward Prescott lived and breathed and slept everything Prescott Holdings and had wanted his sons to do the same. Hunter would admit to working more hours than he probably should, but he did make time to play occasionally. "I'm learning balance." In reality, he was being forced to learn balance.

"That's good to hear. Everything progressing with the resort?"

Annnd, back to business. "Yeah, Dad. Everything is on schedule." His mother joined them and he slung an arm around her shoulders. "I think I'm going to call it a night. Thanks, again, for dinner."

She glanced down at the gold watch on her slender arm. "Oh, it's almost nine. You probably need to go rest."

"Something like that." His plans did include rest, but later. Right now, he needed to see Michaela.

"When are you leaving?"

"Thursday afternoon, but I'll be back in a couple of weeks for the board meeting and to make sure things are still running smoothly with the hospital board."

"Be careful."

He smiled and kissed her cheek. "I'll see you guys later." He sought out Ava, Owen and the kids, said his goodbyes and drove over to Michaela's.

He rang her doorbell and leaned against the column.

Michaela opened the door and her eyes went wide. *"Hunter!"* She launched herself in his arms, then quickly scrambled away from him and ran her hand up and down his arms, as if to steady him. "Oh, I'm sorry. Are you okay?"

Hunter chuckled. "I'm good and I kind of liked that greeting. Makes me think you missed me." It was a good thing he'd had the column to brace against, however, because she had knocked him slightly off balance. The bright smile on her face and her excitement would've been worth the fall.

She pulled him inside and closed the door. "I thought you said you weren't coming back for another two weeks."

"I wanted to surprise you."

"I'm more than surprised. How long are you going to be here?"

"Thursday." He sat on the sofa, pulled her down onto his lap and kissed her. "Do you have any plans for tomorrow evening? I like to have dinner with you."

"No. And I'd love dinner." Michaela bit her lip, as if she wanted to say something else.

"What is it?"

"Can we eat here or at your place? I'm not in the mood to have the entire town interrupting us every five minutes trying to be nosy."

She had a point and more than likely, he'd be the target of more than a few hostile glares and outright nasty comments. Yeah, eating at home would be best. Hunter didn't want to have to risk cussing somebody out. "Definitely. We can figure out the details between now and then."

She nodded and laid her head against his shoulder.

He held her close in his arms for several minutes. "I owe you an apology, Michaela."

She lifted her head and he met her wary gaze.

After all that had happened, he couldn't blame her for the way she looked at him, but he wanted to reassure her they were good. "Everything's okay, sweetheart. I want to tell you how sorry I am for leaving you to deal with this town alone, for the pain and embarrassment I caused you. For everything."

"It was hard, so hard," she whispered.

"I know, baby, and I was so wrong to do that to you."

Hunter alternately wiped and kissed her tears away. "Forgive me." He'd never begged a woman for anything in his life, but if he had to get down on his knees, he would. He rested his forehead against hers. "Please forgive me. I love you and I promise I will never make you cry again. I'll never cause you another moment of pain."

"Yes. I forgive you."

"Thank you," he whispered over and over, placing butterfly kisses all over her face, while his hand slid over her hip, waist and up to cup her breasts. She moaned and her head dropped back. Hunter transferred his kisses to her throat and the portion of her chest left bare by the low-cut tee. "You are so beautiful."

"And so are you." Michaela grabbed his head and pulled him into a soul-stirring kiss.

Arousal began to flow through his body, sending a sharp jolt to his groin. He sat her up, divested her of her shirt and took a moment to just stare at her smooth cocoa skin and sexy red bra.

"Hunter?"

"Yes."

"Make love to me."

Her words were music to his ears and unleashed all the desire that had lain dormant for the past year. "You only have to ask, sweetheart." Michaela stood and held out her hand. He grasped it and rose to his feet in one swift motion, and let her lead him to her bedroom. Once there, he laid her on the bed and took his time removing her clothes, piece by piece, lingering over each part of her body as if it were a priceless artwork. He started at her ankles and kissed his way up one leg and inner thigh, then the other. "I've missed you so much. *So* much." Gently turning her on her stomach, he continued his journey upward. Straddling her hips, he used his tongue to chart a path down the center of her spine.

She moaned loudly. "I missed you, too. Missed the way you touch me."

"I'm going to make up for all of it," he said, trailing his hands everywhere his tongue had been. He massaged every part of her body, then rolled her onto her back again. Cupping her breasts in his hands, he kneaded and massaged them before bending to take one nipple in his mouth. He released one breast and kissed the other while his hand traveled down her flat belly to the softness between her thighs.

Michaela arched off the bed and cried out.

He'd gone without this connection to her for too long. He needed her in his life like he needed to breathe. Going back to her mouth, he slid his tongue between her parted lips, capturing her tongue and absorbing her essence into his very soul. She reached out and unbuttoned his shirt, trailing her hot tongue down his chest as she went and sending sharp jolts of electricity straight to his groin. She pushed it off his shoulders and added it to the growing pile of clothes. Hunter left the bed briefly to finish undressing and don a condom. Coming back to the bed, he kissed his way down to her center, gently spread her legs and swiped his tongue against her clit.

Her hips flew off the bed and she let out a scream. "Hunter!"

He swirled his tongue deeper and deeper inside her, wanting her to remember how it was with them, how it always would be—an all-consuming passion. He took his time, using slow, long licks to increase her pleasure. The sounds of ecstasy spilling from her mouth sent his desire soaring straight through the roof. She erupted with a loud cry, her sounds of pleasure stoking the flames of his arousal even more. He moved up and over her body, taking her mouth in another scorching kiss that made his body tremble right along with hers. He slid two fingers inside her and noted the tight fit.

"There's been no one else. I couldn't...you're the only one I want," Michaela said.

Her words humbled him and made his emotions swell. "And you're the only one I want, the only one I need. There will never be another woman for me. Just you," he said. At the same time, he eased his erection into her sweet warmth, groaning as her tight walls clamped down on him. He thrust in and out with long, deliberate strokes, going deeper each time. His hands roamed possessively over her body as he whispered tender endearments in her ear. He gasped as her feminine muscles clutched him tighter. Hunter rocked into her over and over, varying the length of his strokes, but keeping the same languid tempo. Taking his time and recapturing the love they once shared.

She arched upward and wrapped her legs around him, digging her heels into his back. *"Don't stop."*

"I missed being inside of you like this. I could stay here forever." No other woman came close to making him feel the way she did. Soon, his pace increased, his thrusts deepened and he could sense her on the verge of another orgasm. "Come with me, baby." Her nails dug into his chest and shoulders, and their blended cries echoed throughout the room.

Abruptly, she let out a high-pitched scream as she climaxed all around him, her feminine muscles clenching him tight.

Hunter gripped her hips and growled hoarsely as an explosive orgasm ripped through him with a force that stole his breath and left his entire body shaking. He held her tightly as they both shuddered with the aftershocks. At length their breathing slowed. He rolled to his side, taking her with him. He closed his eyes and idly ran his hands up and down her back.

"Hunter?"

"Hmm."

"How long are you going to stay in California? Are you planning to move back home soon?"

He weighed his words carefully. "I'm going to continue commuting for a while, but I had eventually hoped to stay in LA permanently."

"Where does that leave me? And us?"

"Exactly where you are right now. With me. You asked me when I'd purchased the house during your visit to LA and I told you I had just bought it the month before our wedding was supposed to take place. What I didn't tell you is that I'd bought it for you. It was my wedding gift to you."

Michaela sat up straight. "What did you just say?"

A smile curved his lips. "The house is for you. Do you remember what you said during our weekend getaway there two years ago?"

She eyed him. "No, but apparently you do, since you seem to remember everything I say. I need to watch my mouth around you." He tickled her and she slapped his hand away. "Stop it and just tell me," she said, laughing.

"You said you wouldn't mind moving to LA because of the greater opportunities for art and you loved the beaches."

"That's still true, but what about my job?"

"What about your art?" he countered. "You said that was your dream."

"It is."

"Do you know who Monte is?"

Michaela angled her head. "Is that a trick question? The R&B singer and producer. Of course I know who Monte is with his fine a—."

Hunter narrowed his eyes. "Excuse me?"

She cleared her throat. "I mean the man can really sing. Um…so what about him?"

"I talked to Eric yesterday and Monte is producing his band's album."

"That's great for Eric, but what does that have to do with me?"

He sighed in exasperation. "If you stop interrupting me, I can finish." She mimicked zipping her lips and he chuckled. "I don't know what I'm going to do with you. Anyway, Monte's wife is an artist and Monte said he'd be more than happy to arrange for the two of you to meet and talk."

Michaela's eyes widened and her mouth fell open. She slowly brought her hands to her mouth and fell back against the pillows. Then she popped back up. "Are you *kidding me*? This isn't a joke, right, Hunter?"

"I wouldn't do that to you, baby. I have his number and we can call to set up a visit whenever you're ready."

"I'm ready *now*," she said, grinning and bouncing up and down like an excited kid.

He exploded with laughter. Seeing her happy made everything in his world right again. She was his. Forever.

CHAPTER 6

Two weeks had passed since Michaela's conversation with Hunter. She was almost finished with her murals and she couldn't wait for everyone to see them at the unveiling scheduled in two weeks. This was also her last week of vacation and if she were being honest, she'd admit to not missing her job at all. Come to think of it, it hadn't crossed her mind once and she wondered if it might be time for a career move, after all. As nervous as she felt about just outright quitting her job, she'd had him call and set up the meeting with Monte's wife.

When they arrived at the airport for their early Saturday morning flight, it surprised her to see Hunter request the wheelchair, and she could tell by the tightness of his jaw that he was uncomfortable with her seeing him this way. She imagined having to rush across an airport would be tiring for him. "Ready?"

He whipped his head around and stared up at her. "What are you doing?"

"Getting ready to give you the ride of your life," she said and tossed him a bold wink. "I can make it fast or...," She leaned down close to his ear and whispered seductively, "I can take it *real* slow."

Desire flared in his eyes. "Be careful or I'm going to be the one taking *you* fast *and* slow."

And I'd let you. Right here. Right now. Heat spread through her body. Michaela didn't say anything. She concentrated on getting them through the TSA checkpoint and to the gate without finding a spot to let him do exactly as he'd said.

Without any delays, they made it to LA around noon, rented a car and drove to his house. Michaela could see that the flight had taken a lot out of Hunter as he slowly climbed the stairs and trudged down the hallway to the master bedroom. She sat on the bed and patted the space next to her.

Hunter came and joined her. "Nervous?"

"A little. But you'll be with me, so I'll be okay. Right now, you need to rest. You don't have to pretend with me, Hunter," she added when he started to protest. She leaned her head against his shoulder. "You're tired, baby. We have a good five hours before we have to leave, so there's plenty of time."

He placed a soft kiss on her forehead. "I know. It's just frustrating."

"It won't be like this always. You're getting stronger every day and needing that cane less and less." She knew he didn't like showing his weaknesses, especially in front of her. "Pretty soon, you're going to be running marathons without breaking a sweat."

Grinning, he said, "Thank you." He kicked off his shoes and stretched out across the bed, face down. "I only need a couple of hours."

"Okay." She lay next to him and ran a comforting hand up and down his back. A few minutes later, his breathing became deep and even. He'd fallen asleep. Michaela eased off the bed and went to stand on the balcony. The early March temperatures hovered in the low seventies and a slight breeze blew across her face. She closed her eyes and tried to still the butterflies fluttering around in her belly. *I can do this. This is my dream.* She made a mental list of the questions she wanted to ask Janae and hoped she could remember them all.

Going back inside, she went downstairs. On her first visit, she had been so angry that she never took the invited tour. The second time, she had been so focused on getting her apology out that she'd only done a quick walk-through. She still marveled at the fact that he'd bought the house for her. Smiling, she hummed Salt-N-Pepa's "Whatta Man" as she walked through the home with its highly polished wood floors, reverently running her hand over the dark marble counter in the gourmet kitchen with its two islands. The living, dining and family rooms had all been elegantly furnished, but still felt warm and inviting. Michaela noticed a partially walled off area between the dining room and kitchen. *How did I miss this last time?* Curious, she entered the space. Although the two walls of window offered nice views of the ocean, this space had the most spectacular one of all. It had been left empty, but had track lighting and built in shelving and cabinets. *What's he going to put in here?* Leaving the area, she found a home gym and a smaller room next to it holding a hospital bed. He must have spent his time there when he couldn't climb the stairs. The sight made her heart hurt all over again. She sent up a prayer of thanks that he no longer needed that bed and another one that he never would again.

Reversing her steps, she went back upstairs. The master bedroom was located on one side and she found three other bedrooms and two bathrooms on the opposite side. None were furnished. Michaela tipped back into the bedroom and found Hunter still asleep. She crossed the room to the master bath. *Wow.* The bathtub looked big enough to swim in and the shower wide enough for at least three people comfortably. She started humming the song again on her way out. "Yes, he is," she said softly.

Still in awe, she walked back into the room and went still. Hanging over the bed, was the painting of a sunrise that she'd done for Mr. Prescott. She had wondered what happened to it, but was ecstatic that it hadn't been lost. She retrieved her art pad and colored pencils and took a seat on the lounger next to the window. Her hand flew across the page as the sketch came to life.

"Hey, baby." Hunter pressed a kiss to Michaela's neck.

She jumped slightly. "Hey. How was your nap?"

"Good. I'm starving, though." He sat next to her and studied her drawing. "I like it."

"Thanks." Michaela studied the abstract. "It's not done yet, but I like it, too." She pointed to the painting over the bed. "It looks good in here."

He followed where she gestured. "Granddad left it to me because he knew I would treasure it."

This man is going to make me fall even deeper in love with him, and I don't know how that's possible. She leaned over and kissed his bearded cheek. "I'm glad you have it. I was hoping someone hadn't taken it. Do you want to go out to get something to eat?" she asked, going back to the previous conversation.

"No. I can fix us something light. It's after three and we're having dinner at six, so it doesn't make sense to have a big meal." Monte and his wife had invited them to dinner at their home, rather than meeting at a restaurant.

"I still can't believe they invited us to their home." She was going to have to try to act like she had some sense and not go all fangirl crazy. *Like maybe I can pull that off. Yeah, right.* She set her pad and pencils aside. "Let's go raid the kitchen." Together, they made turkey sandwiches, added a few chips and drank lemonade.

"You want anything else?" Hunter asked after they finished.

"Nope. I'm good. I do have a question, though. What's going to be in that large space in the corner with the track lighting?" She hopped down from the barstool and walked over.

He followed and placed his arms around her waist. "This is the place I had renovated for your art studio. It has the most panoramic view of the ocean and I thought it would perfect."

"Oh, my goodness." Michaela could immediately see herself spending hours here. He'd told her he loved her, and continued to show her in every way. "Thank you, thank you." She pulled his head down and crushed her mouth against his, wanting him to know how much he meant to her. It didn't take much for desire to explode and she found herself against the wall.

"I think I want that ride now," Hunter murmured, while easing her knit pants and panties down. "I can't think of a more perfect way to christen this spot, to start with the passion that I know you'll bring to every masterpiece you create."

His fingers went to her core, causing a flurry of sensations to flow through her. Her hands slid beneath his shirt to touch his bare skin and she felt the muscles of his abs contract. He captured her mouth in another scorching kiss, this one more intense than the previous one. They both moaned. She reached for his belt, undid it, unzipped his pants and pushed them down.

"This ride is going to have to be fast."

Hallelujah! She just needed him inside her now. "I'm still on the pill." She'd begun taking them a few months before their wedding and they had pretty much stopped using condoms after that point. "I want to feel all of you."

"Michaela."

The tenderness and love she saw reflected in his eyes nearly did her in. Then his gaze changed, and a wicked gleam appeared in his eyes. Her pulse skipped.

Hunter drove into her with one long thrust. "Get ready to ride."

Michaela wrapped her arms around his neck and locked her legs around his back as he set a hard, driving rhythm had her holding on tight. She arched and writhed against him as he pumped faster, delving deeper with each thrust. He whispered a mixture of tender endearments and erotic promises that made her desire climb even higher. Their breathing grew louder as he gripped her tighter and stroked her harder. He had every nerve in her body electrified. The pressure built inside her with an intensity she'd never felt, and she convulsed and screamed his name as waves of ecstasy crashed through her so violently she thought she might pass out.

He drove into her faster and moments later, he went rigid, threw his head back and exploded, yelling out her name. "Damn, girl." He rested his head against hers, their breathing ragged. "Thanks for the ride."

"Any time," she said with a tired laugh. "I sure hope we didn't give your neighbors a show." She'd completely forgotten about the wall of windows.

"It's one-way glass."

"Thank goodness."

Hunter chuckled and slowly lowered her to the floor. "Let's hit the shower."

An hour later, her body still hummed as they followed directions to Monte's home. They had to stop at a gate and call to gain entry.

"Nice area," Hunter said.

"Very." Those doggone butterflies were back and tap

dancing in her belly like they were a Gregory Hines protégé. He parked, helped her out of the car and held her hand as they approached the door.

The door opened seconds after Hunter rang the bell. "You must be Hunter and Michaela. Please come in. It's nice to meet you both."

Hunter nodded and shook Monte's hand. "Same here." He stepped back for Michaela to enter first.

Michaela forgot to breathe. She was standing in *Monte's house*. When she finally found her voice, she said, "Okay, I'm sorry, but I'ma need about thirty seconds to fangirl. I can't believe I'm meeting Monte! Can I get a picture, please? Oh, and don't worry, I won't put it on social media. I know how you are about your privacy."

"Sure," Monte said with a chuckle, apparently used to the fanfare.

She did a little squeal, whipped out her phone and handed it to Hunter. "Can you take the picture, babe?"

Hunter shook his head, snapped the picture and gave her the phone.

She looked at the photo. "Melanie and Lana are going to flip. Thank you so much, Monte."

"At home, I'm just Terrence," he said. "Come on back so you can meet Janae."

She smiled up at Hunter and he whispered, "You're not supposed to ask your man to take a picture of you with another man. Don't you know that?"

"Oops, my bad?"

"Yeah, oops, *yo'* bad."

She giggled when he rolled his eyes. "I don't plan to touch anybody but you, so no worries. And I'm thinking another ride would be good…fast or slow, your choice."

"You really like tempting me, don't you?"

"Me? I don't know what you mean.," Michaela said innocently, then turned in time to see Janae enter.

"Hunter and Michaela, I'd like you to meet my wife, Janae Campbell."

Janae smiled warmly. "It's so nice to meet you both."

"It's a pleasure to meet you, too," Hunter said.

Michaela shook the woman's extended hand. The beautiful petite woman had to be a good three or four inches shorter than Michaela's own five-five height. "Likewise, Mrs. Campbell. You have a lovely home and your children are simply beautiful." The large framed photo of a little girl, who looked to be around three, kissing her infant brother, hung in the living room over the fireplace.

"Call me Janae, and thank you. They're a handful, but my parents are in town this weekend and they volunteered to babysit overnight, so you won't get to meet them. I hope you're hungry. Terrence made my favorite meal—lobster, crab and asparagus over penne pasta and his homemade French bread."

She tried to hide her look of surprise. The man was a mega-star and he cooked dinner.

Janae must have seen it because she said laughingly, "I know. I felt the same way when I found out he cooks. He's way better at it than me, so I just step back and let him do his thing. As a matter of fact, what we're having is the first meal he prepared for me. That's why it's my favorite." She gazed up at Terrance with adoring eyes and he placed a tender kiss on her lips.

"You know I enjoy cooking for you, sweetheart," Terrence said with the same love shining his eyes.

The love between them was so strong, Michaela felt like she was intruding on a private moment. The couple led them into a dining room set with elegant African motif china and cloth napkins. Once the food had been brought out and everyone served, conversation flowed around the table as if they were old friends. "Terrence, this food is so good, and this bread is to die for."

"The bread is my grandmother's recipe. My grandparents live in the connected cottage. I would introduce you, but she hasn't been feeling the best."

She could see the pain reflected in his face. He was obviously very close them. "I hope she feels better very soon."

"Thank you."

"So, Michaela, I hear you're interested in pursuing art," Janae said.

"I am. Right now I'm finishing up a commissioned mural for our hospital's new cancer wing, but the day job will be calling me back in a week. Are you an artist full-time?"

"I am. I worked as a special education teacher in San Jose, but when we got married, Terrence convinced me to try my hand at doing art, instead of looking for a new position here. It was the best decision I've ever made."

"Hunter has been saying the same thing."

"Girl, then what are you waiting for? If you have a man who loves you and encourages you to pursue your passion, go for it. I'll be happy to help you in any way I can."

Michaela shared a look with Hunter and he gave her a nod of support. Could she walk away from a secure career into the unknown? The thought made her almost hyperventilate. She felt the gentle squeeze on her hand from Hunter. *Yeah, I can do this.*

~

Hunter stared around at the crowded room filled with dignitaries, hospital board members and everyone else who had come to see the unveiling of Michaela's murals. He was probably just as anxious as she. His parents, Ava and Owen had all come to show their support. He spotted Cooper—who was miraculously still in town—across the room with a woman. *I definitely need to see what's up with that.* He scanned the area, searching for his woman. His heart nearly beat out of his chest when he saw her laughing with her mother and her two friends, Melanie and Lana. He loved her so damn much, it scared him sometimes, but he didn't plan to let that fear or anything else stop him from keeping her in his life this time. *Every sunrise is an opportunity for a new start. Make each one count.* His grandfather's words had played over in his head since returning from LA last weekend. If he didn't know better, he'd think the old man was orchestrating things from heaven. *Yeah, Granddad is doing this. He even said she's the one for me.* Granddad provided the opportunity and Hunter had capitalized on it. He had fixed it.

Crossing the room, he joined Michaela's group.

"Hunter it's so good to see you," Mrs. Saunders said, hugging him. Then she whispered for his ears only, "I'm so glad to see you and my baby together again. Take advantage of this second chance. Not everyone gets one."

"You're right and I promise I will." Behind the happiness, Hunter could see the pain and knew it stemmed from the loss of her husband. "Ladies." He kissed the cheeks of Lana and Melanie.

"Hey, Hunter," they chorused.

The fact that they weren't shooting daggers his way told him that Michaela had told them some, if not all of what happened. He slid his arm around Michaela's waist. She looked stunning in a black halter dress that hugged her enticing curves and had twisted her shoulder-length hair into an elaborate updo. "Have I told you how gorgeous you look tonight?"

Michaela made a show of thinking. "Only about eight or nine times. You're way behind, so I'm going to need you to step it up a little more." She gave him the smile he knew was meant just for him.

"Ladies and gentlemen, may I have your attention, please?" It took a minute or two for the conversations to drop to a murmur, then stop altogether. "We are so excited that you're here for the grand opening of the Abraham T. Prescott Cancer Center." Deafening applause sounded around the room and the board's chairman had to wait for the audience to settle down, once again. "Ms. Saunders, will you join me, please?"

Hunter released her and gestured her forward.

"You aren't coming with me?" she asked.

"This is your night, baby. I'll be right here. Go ahead."

Michaela strutted up to the front, causing more than a few male heads to turn. The chairman handed her the microphone. "Thank you all for coming. I was honored when Mr. Prescott asked me to paint these murals and I wanted to create something that will, hopefully, give all those who come through these doors a little beauty and peace." She nodded and the drapes came down.

A collective gasp went up around the room, then the applause began and rose, once again, to deafening levels. Hunter had never seen anything more amazing and his chest pounded with pride. She had chosen two beach scenes, but they differed in tone. The adult side showed a wooden pathway leading to the beach, with benches placed along the way for someone to sit and enjoy the beauty and, yes, peace. In contrast, the children's mural had a playful theme, with sandcastles, buckets, seashells and butterflies. Michaela still hadn't made a decision, but he had no doubt that if she decided to quit her job, she would have a very successful art career.

It was more than an hour later before Hunter had a chance to talk to Michaela. She had been mobbed from the moment the murals were revealed. "I'm so proud of you, sweetheart."

"Do you like them?"

"Like them? I absolutely love them. And I love you." Before he had a chance to say anything else, his family approached.

Ava grabbed Michaela in a big hug. "Girlfriend, those paintings are fabulous. Granddad knew exactly what he was doing."

"Thanks, Ava. It's good to see you all again," Michaela said.

His mother grasped Michaela's hands. "You did an amazing job. Just outstanding!"

His father hugged her. "Dad would be so proud."

"Thank you for saying that, Mr. Prescott. I really hope so." Michaela dabbed at a tear.

They stood around talking for another few minutes, but Hunter was anxious to leave so they could have their own private celebration. "Finally," he muttered when the last stragglers trudged out the door.

Once they made it back to his condo, Michaela let out a scream. "I can't believe it! They loved it. Oh, my goodness, I was so nervous." She did a happy dance.

Laughing, he said, "I don't know why. You have a gift, a rare and precious gift that needs to be shared to infuse beauty into this, sometimes, harsh world." He knew and understood what her gift could do. Her paintings had been one of the things that pushed him harder on days when he wanted to give up.

"You're right." She squared her shoulders. "I've made my decision. I want to do this, Hunter. I'm ready to take the risk. To move to California, live in that beautiful house and see if I can't make this work."

He smiled and drew her into his arms. "That sounds wonderful, but there's one problem."

"What?" she asked, frowning.

"That house was built for my wife, and the only woman who'll reside there is her."

Her eyes went wide. "Are you saying what I think you're saying?"

"I am." Hunter lowered himself to one knee. "We've been given a second chance and I want to make every one of these moments count. This time, we will be a team and, no matter what storms life throws at us, we'll weather them *together*. Will you marry—"

"*Yes, yes, yes!*"

He rose to his feet and sealed their agreement with a kiss. "Oh, Granddad left another envelope for you." He walked over to the kitchen counter, where he'd placed it, came back and handed it to her.

Michaela tore into it and pulled out the sheet of paper. A check floated to the floor. She stooped to picked it up. "*Ohmigod, fifty thousand dollars!*" She read the note out loud. "Michaela, thank you for honoring the request of this old man. I only wish I were there to see it. The check is for your commission fee and I included a little extra to help you get started on your art career. You and Hunter have a wonderful life together. Love, Granddad." She burst out laughing around her tears. "He knew we needed each other more than we did. The first letter said you were the one for me."

"He said the same thing in mine." And he was happy to say he'd gotten his life together and honored every one of his grandfather's wishes.

EPILOGUE

One month later...

Hunter stood in the backyard at Prescott Manor awaiting his bride. They'd decided to forego a large wedding and, instead, have a small one with just their family and close friends. When she appeared, it took everything in him to stand still. He didn't think she could improve on perfection, but the ivory strapless gown she wore, did exactly that, emphasizing her full breasts, small waist and flaring hips. It wasn't until he was halfway down the aisle that he realized his feet were moving.

"What the hell is he doing?" Hunter heard Maverick say.

Hunter was going to meet his baby, so she would know she'd never walk alone again. She gave him a soft smile and took his extended arm. Together, they strolled back up the aisle to where the minister awaited. Ten minutes later, he heard the words he'd been waiting for, the ones he should have heard more than a year ago.

"I now pronounce you husband and wife. Hunter, you make kiss your bride."

He seized her mouth in a searing kiss before the man

finished, pouring everything he felt for her in it, wanting her to know that from now on this was how it would be between them. And he wanted their first kiss as husband and wife to be filled with love and anticipation of what was to come.

"I love you, Hunter."

"And I love you, Mrs. Prescott."

"I'm thinking I'd like to go for another ride tonight."

He raised an eyebrow. "Is that right? Well, since it's our wedding night, your wish is my command. Would you like it fast or slow?"

"I was thinking maybe we can start slow and end fast," Michaela said seductively.

"If you're not careful, you'll be getting that ride sooner, rather than later." He grew up in this house and knew every private spot.

She gave him a careless shrug. "Whenever you're ready, just say the word."

"I think you like tempting me."

"Maybe, but I'm more than capable of backing it up."

Hunter felt himself becoming aroused and decided they needed to table the conversation and mingle with their guests.

"We make the best team," Michaela said, smiling up at him as they started toward their families.

"The best." Hunter glanced around at all the familiar faces and finally understood his grandfather's words. Though he still needed to maintain a level of privacy, the woman standing at his side and his family was *home*, no matter where he lived. *My heart is home.*

ACKNOWLEDGMENTS

My Heavenly Father, thank you for my life and for loving me better than I can love myself.

To my husband, Lance, you will always be my #1 hero!

To my children, family and friends, thank you for your continued support. I appreciate and love you!

To my series sisters - Sherelle, Leslie and Angela, you already know how much I adore you ladies!

Brandi, you are a lifesaver!! I love you.

A very special thank you to the Prince of Sophisticated Soul, Will Downing, for taking time to share your journey and for more than 30 years of the best music. Much love to you!

Thank you to all the readers who have supported and encouraged me. I couldn't do this without you.

DEAR READER

Dear Reader ~

I hope you enjoyed Hunter and Michaela's second chance journey to love, forgiveness and acceptance. Sometimes, things aren't always the way they seem, especially when life changes in an instant. Believe me, I know! And when it's a debilitating disease, it can be even more challenging to find the way back. To find out more information about Polymyositis, visit https://www.myositis.org.

Thank you for taking this ride with me and be sure to let me know your thoughts at sheryllister@gmail.com.

Love & Blessings,
Sheryl

When the powerful patriarch of the Prescott family dies, four brothers are challenged to return to Rosewood Heights and fulfill their grandfather's last wishes. With each of these compelling and complex men facing their inner demons, they must ask themselves if light can shine in the midst of tragedy and if home is truly where the heart is...

Finding Cooper by Elle Wright: bit.ly/FindingCooperEW
Inspiring Dominic by Sherelle Green:
bit.ly/InspiringDominicSG
Craving Maverick by Angela Seals:
bit.ly/CravingMaverickAS

EXCERPT FROM HER PASSIONATE PROMISE

Eric Dawson leaned back in his chair and stretched to relieve the kinks in his neck. For the balance of his day, he'd been working on a class action suit filed by residents of an apartment complex, citing the owner's neglect to address a mold issue.

"You're still here?"

He shifted his gaze to the door where his colleague and friend, Jamal Montgomery stood. "Yeah, man." The two had met in law school and ended up at the same firm. "I could ask you the same question."

Something like a shadow passed over Jamal's face. "No reason to go home, since my wife is working late."

"Problems?"

"Feels like it sometimes. Are you playing tonight?" Jamal asked, changing the subject.

Eric nodded. "Which is why I need to pack up and leave." He and a group of friends had formed a band five years ago and spent many of their weekends playing at small clubs, restaurants and private parties. "We're playing at a club in Santa Monica. Why don't you drop in, have a drink and listen to the first set. Asia should be home by the time it's over."

"That would be nice. It would be even nicer if she were coming with me," he added wryly.

Eric stood. "Next time. We'll be there for the next several weekends, so you have plenty of opportunities to bring her. You guys can have dinner on me." He closed up the files, shoved them in his briefcase and did the same with his laptop.

"What time does the first set start?"

"Seven-thirty." They stepped out into the hallway and Eric locked the door.

Jamal checked his watch. "That gives me two and a half hours. I'll probably do a little more research on the mold case, then come on over."

He gave Jamal the name and address of the club. "See you in a while." They did a fist bump and went in opposite directions.

It took him more than half an hour to drive from Manhattan Beach to his home in Marina Del Rey. *Not bad for a Friday.* Eric leafed through the mail he'd collected from the box and, not seeing anything urgent, tossed the pile on the kitchen bar. He stopped by his home office and dropped off the briefcase before retracing his steps to the kitchen to heat up a meal from one of those online meal planning services. He preferred cooking for himself, but between the long hours he put in at the law firm and his music, these days, he rarely had an opportunity to do so. His grandfather had been on him lately about slowing down and taking time to relax and enjoy life. Eric enjoyed his life fine, but he needed to stay busy. It kept the demons at bay. Thinking about his grandfather reminded Eric that he hadn't checked on the old man in a couple of weeks. He'd stop by for a visit before tomorrow's show.

He finished his food, then climbed the stairs to his bedroom for a quick shower. Twenty minutes later, he was on his way to Infuse Rhythm Lounge, the one place that gave him a measure of peace. Upon arrival, Eric felt the week's tension drain from his body.

"Hey, Eric. Looking forward to some good music tonight. You sure I can't convince you to meet my niece, Candice. She just graduated from nursing school."

"Hi, Ms. Della, and no matchmaking. I'm not looking for a hookup or anything else," Eric added with a chuckle. The older woman worked as the hostess for the restaurant and had been trying to introduce him to one niece after the other since the band started playing there three months ago.

"Pity," she said with a smile.

He just shook his head and maneuvered his way through a small knot of people gathered on one side of the bar and signaled the bartender.

"My man, Big E. Your usual?"

Eric nodded and slid onto one of the barstools just vacated by a couple. While waiting, he checked the time. He still had a good forty-five minutes before showtime, so it gave him a few minutes for a drink. He threw up a wave to the band members seated at a table finishing dinner. They had sent him a text earlier inviting him, but he'd had to decline. The bartender placed the whiskey neat in front of Eric. "Thanks, Mike." He pushed a bill toward the man, then picked up the glass. Most of the band members had a tab opened for the evening, but Eric limited himself to one drink.

Before he got two sips in, a woman came over, openly flirting and trying to engage him in a conversation. It took a minute, but she finally realized he wasn't interested and moved on. A second woman approached shortly after and his message was the same—not interested. He just wanted to be left alone to enjoy his drink. It didn't take her long to get the message, either. Relaxing, he brought the glass to his lips, but went still when he saw the woman who'd been coming on to him for the past few weeks approaching. He sighed.

Mike chuckled. "Popular man tonight."

Eric shot him a look.

"Looking good, Eric," she said, giving him a coy smile.

For the life of him, he couldn't remember her name. She didn't seem to notice his lack of response.

"I love the way your hands move up and down that saxophone." She leaned closer and placed her hand on his thigh. "Makes me wonder how it would feel to have you do the same thing to me."

He removed the hand that had started moving upward, drained the contents of the glass and stood. "I'm not interested. I need to get ready for the show. Enjoy your evening." Without a backward glance, Eric walked away. There was a long list of women drawn to his success and money, but if he let his dick lead him where his mind told him not to go, he'd be without both. And he had more sense than that. Or at least he did now. An image of his ex flashed in his head and he quickly shoved it aside and greeted the band members coming toward the stage. The five men had been childhood friends and played in the school's band. Even though they'd drifted apart during their college years, their friendship and mutual love of music had brought them back together. Calvin, the keyboardist, had been a session musician for several popular jazz artists and suggested the group form a band during one of their meetups four years ago. Everyone had agreed. Initially, they had only been able to get a few gigs here and there, but over the past several months, the requests had increased and they were booked through the half the summer.

They went through the routine of tuning the instruments and at exactly seven-thirty, the announcer joined them.

"Welcome to Infuse Rhythm Lounge, where good food and great music rule. Tonight, we are excited to have Virtual Soul back with us." Applause and whistles filled the room and the woman waited until it died down before continuing. "Before I turn the stage over to them, there are a couple of house rules to remember—absolutely no flash photography and no recording of the show. Now, put your hands together for Virtual Soul!"

On the heels of her words, the band launched into their first song. As the notes from his sax filled the room and his soul, Eric lost himself in the music. This was where he wanted to be, *needed* to be—in the place as essential to him as breathing and where he could shut out the memories that threatened to drown him most days. His solace.

~

Kathi parked in front of her grandmother's house, got out and started up the walk. She didn't think she would ever get used to the traffic in LA. It had taken her almost twenty minutes to go nine miles. She smiled when the door opened and her grandmother rushed out to meet Kathi with a hug. At age seventy-one, Estelle McBride could still turn the heads of men with her trim body. She barely had wrinkles on her mocha colored face. That old adage about "good Black don't crack" came to mind.

"Oh, I'm so glad to see you, baby. How are you?" she asked, leading Kathi inside and to the kitchen.

"I'm good." Kathi glanced around at the foil covered dishes lining the counter. "Um…Grandma, I thought we were just having lunch." She peeked inside and found barbeque chicken, baked beans, potato salad and the homemade rolls that Kathi loved. "And this is way too much food for two people."

Her grandmother carried over a glass dish and placed it next to the other ones. "It's not just for two people. I invited Charles to join us."

She went still. Ever since she moved to LA, Estelle had been subtly matchmaking, telling her *just because you skinned your knee doesn't mean you don't try again.* "Um…who's Charles?" A soft moan escaped when she realized the dish held another of her favorites—peach cobbler. Kathi was going to seriously hurt herself eating and hoped there would be enough for at least one to-go plate.

"He's a wonderful man I met three months ago." She pulled Kathi out to the dining room and picked up her phone. "I promised your mother I'd get a picture of you, so she'd know you were okay."

Laughing, Kathi said, "I just talked to her a week and a half ago."

"Okay, I'm ready. Let's do a selfie." She paused. "Wait, an *us*-ie. That's the correct term, right?"

"Yes, Grandma." They posed for the picture and she smiled watching her send it in a text to her mother. Glynda Norris had been heartbroken when Kathi decided to move. As an only child, Kathi and her mother had been joined at the hip since birth and, even though Kathi was thirty-three, she guessed old habits were hard to break. She opened her mouth to ask about Charles again and the doorbell rang.

"Oh, that must be Charles," her grandmother gushed and hurried off.

Great. She would play nice long enough to consume what would be the best meal she'd had since leaving Portland, then make an excuse to leave. She wanted the love of a good man who wasn't afraid of long-term commitment and refused to settle for less. She didn't think a blind date fell into that category. A moment later, she heard male laughter. *Nice voice.*

"Kathi, I'd like you to meet Charles Dawson. Charles, my granddaughter, Kathi Norris."

It took a minute for Kathi to find her voice. The man standing before her was close to six feet, had a handsome coffee colored face and salt and pepper hair. Her grandmother held a small bouquet of roses. It finally clicked. Charles was here for her grandmother, not Kathi. She smiled and extended her hand. "It's so nice to meet you, Mr. Dawson."

"It's nice to finally meet you, too. Your grandmother has told me a lot about you."

"Really?" Kathi glanced over at her grandmother. She hadn't seen the woman smile this bright since before Kathi's grandfather died ten years ago. *Yeah, we have some catching up to do.*

"Oh, yes. She's really proud of you." Mr. Dawson gave her grandmother's waist an affectionate squeeze. "It smells good in here, Stelle."

"I hope it tastes just as good. You all come on and eat."

They grabbed plates from the table, filled their plates in the kitchen then came back to the dining room.

"I forgot to bring the iced tea," her grandmother said.

Mr. Dawson stood. "I'll get it, sweetheart." He disappeared around the corner into the kitchen.

Kathi leaned forward and whispered, "You've been holding out on me. I want to know all about where you found Mr. Hot Chocolate."

Estelle giggled and blushed like a schoolgirl. She waved a hand. "We'll talk about it later," she said with a wink.

Kathi's mouth fell open. Before she could comment, Mr. Dawson came back with the tea and poured some in each of their glasses. He recited a short blessing and they dug in.

After her first bite of a roll, it took everything in Kathi not to moan and swoon under the table. Evidently she didn't do a good job of hiding her reaction because her grandmother chuckled.

"You always did love those rolls. I made an extra pan for you to take home."

Kathi smiled. "You're the best grandma ever."

"Charles, when Kathi was little, she'd eat at least five of those rolls. I always wondered where she put them with her itty bitty self."

He laughed and held up a roll. "Kathi, I don't blame you. I'd like to put away five, myself, but the old body won't let me enjoy myself like I used to."

"Neither will mine," Kathi said. Conversation flowed around the table and she found out that Mr. Dawson had worked as an engineer before retiring and that his wife died of a massive stroke sixteen years ago. "How did you two meet?"

"Through mutual friends at a surprise birthday party. When your grandmother walked into the room, I lost my train of thought and couldn't remember my name."

"You remembered it fine by the time you came over to introduce yourself," her grandmother teased.

Mr. Dawson squeezed Estelle's hand. "I had to before some other fella beat me to it."

The loving stare the two of them shared made Kathi feel like she was intruding on a private moment. She couldn't ever remember her ex looking at her that way...unless he wanted something, namely sex. Thinking back, she'd gone along with the stagnant relationship far longer than she should have and he couldn't understand why they needed to change things. She wanted children, but only with a husband. When he suggested they move in together and have a child sans wedding ring, she had walked. Her grandmother's voice brought her back to the conversation.

"Has your lightheadedness gone away?"

He shook his head. "It comes and goes. I'm planning to make an appointment with the doctor."

"Kathi's a doctor."

"I'm a pharmacist," Kathi said with a smile. "Not quite the same. Do you take any medication, Mr. Dawson?"

"About five or six—for high blood pressure, stomach problems and a couple other things—but I can't remember the names offhand. I just know when to take them."

"Kathi, do you think you could check to see if the medications are okay for him?" Her grandmother turned to Mr. Dawson. "I had her look at mine and realized I was still taking stuff I didn't need to. I wonder if that's the same for you."

"His doctor would be the one to discontinue or change the medication, but I'd be more than happy to provide some information about the medications when you have the time." In her mind, Kathi wondered if he was indeed taking more medication than necessary. While she wholeheartedly agreed that medicine was crucial in some instances, she also knew that the older population was sometimes overmedicated.

"I live about five minutes from here and you can follow me home after we leave, if you're not busy."

Estelle touched his arm. "Oh, that's a great idea. Do you have anything planned for later, dear?"

Kathi shook her head. "No. Nothing." The only thing remotely social she had done since coming to the city was attend a memorial. A sad testimonial, but true. She needed to get out more. Conversation continued to flow around the table and, after the food settled, her grandmother served the warm peach cobbler with some homemade vanilla ice cream. Kathi could eat this every day. Of course, she'd have to spend every day in the fitness center located in Park Manor to offset the calories, but it would be oh so worth it.

After finishing, she told her grandmother she'd be back for her rolls and followed Mr. Dawson the short distance to his house. Inside the one-story home, he led her to the family room located at the back of the house.

"Have a seat and I'll get the bottles."

She sat on the sofa glanced around the room. A photo of a beautiful woman, who had to be his late wife hung on the wall. She saw several others of a couple with a young boy at various ages.

"These are all of them."

Kathi took the bottles and read each one. "Do you take any other over-the-counter-medications, like aspirin or herbal supplements?"

"I have a bit of arthritis and I take Ibuprofen for that, especially when the weather changes. But since it's warmer now, I haven't taken it as often."

She wondered if taking the multiple drugs had somehow caused an interaction. The same doctor had prescribed all of them, which puzzled her even more. However, it wasn't her place to tell him whether to stop or change anything, so she chose her next words carefully. "I'd like you to follow up with your doctor and make sure all of these are still good for you to take." Kathi smiled. "As we get older or our internal systems change, sometimes the types of medications or dosages may need to be adjusted." She placed the bottles on the table.

"I'll do that. I appreciate you coming over. I never knew that about medication. With the doctors always rushing in and out, I hardly have time to get a word in. But, this time, he's going to have to slow down and—"

"Gramps, are you back here?"

Kathi turned at the sound of a voice as smooth as black

velvet. The same could be said about its owner when he appeared. She felt a whisper of recognition, and it took her a moment to realize that the cute little boy in the pictures hanging on the wall had grown into a heart-stopping Adonis. He had the same coffee-colored skin tone as his grandfather. With his towering height, dark, piercing eyes and slim, muscular build, she was certain women fell in his path wherever he went. Even she had trouble taking her eyes off him. Kathi shook herself mentally.

"Hey, son." Mr. Dawson engulfed the man in an affectionate hug. "Kathi, this is my grandson, Eric. Eric this is Kathi Norris."

Eric's gaze traveled slowly down her body and back up and his gaze locked on hers. For a split second she saw what looked like interest...attraction? But it was gone so fast, she might have imagined it. She didn't imagine her response, however—the sudden skip in her pulse and the warmth flowing through her. Kathi stopped staring long enough to extend her hand. "It's very nice to meet you, Eric."

"He's a little old for you, don't you think?" Eric said.

Mr. Dawson swung his shocked gaze Eric's way. "Eric!"

Her hand slowly dropped and she eyed him critically. "Did you wake up on the wrong side of the bed today or is that how you usually respond during an introduction? Usually, when a person says nice to meet you, the appropriate reply is 'nice to meet you, too', 'the pleasure is all mine', or something of that nature." Mr. Dawson's eyes widened and he chuckled, but she wasn't finished. "I'm certain you didn't inherit those manners from your grandfather because he's a perfect gentleman." She shifted her gaze to the older man. "I know you'd like to visit with your grandson, so I'll get out of your way." She was so mad, she wanted to punch Eric's lights out. He'd made an assumption about her without even knowing her.

Mr. Dawson sent a disappointed look Eric's way and shook his head. "I'm going to walk Kathi to the door and be right back." Once at the door, he said, "I'm sorry about my grandson. He's usually not like that and I can't figure out why he behaved this way today."

"It's okay." It wasn't, but Mr. Dawson hadn't been the rude one. "Let me know how everything goes."

"I will and thank you again. Tell Stelle, I'll call her later."

Smiling, she said, "I will." When Kathi got into her car, she leaned against the seat. Eric's lack of manners shouldn't have mattered to her one way or the other because she wouldn't have to deal with the man, but for some crazy reason it did.

ABOUT THE AUTHOR

Sheryl Lister is a multi-award-winning author and has enjoyed reading and writing for as long as she can remember. She is a former pediatric occupational therapist with over twenty years of experience, and resides in California. Sheryl is a wife, mother of three daughters and a son-in-love, and grandmother to two special little boys. When she's not writing, Sheryl can be found on a date with her husband or in the kitchen creating appetizers. For more information, visit her website at www.sheryllister.com.

Love's Sweet Kiss (Sassy Seasoned Sisters #1)

Never Letting Go (Carnivale Chronicles)

Embracing Ever After (Once Upon a Baby #1)

Do Me (Irresistible Husband)

Five Midnight Moments (New Year Bae-Solutions)

Made in the USA
Coppell, TX
01 July 2022